Not So Heartwarming Stories

By
Arran Gimba

Not So Heartwarming Stories

This book is a work of fiction. Names, characters, places, and incidents either are products of the author's imagination or are used fictitiously. Any resemblance to actual persons, living or dead, events, or locales is entirely coincidental.

www.arrangimba.com

"Once you've ruled out the impossible then whatever is left, however improbable, must be the truth. The problem lay in working out what was impossible, of course..."

– Terry Pratchett

Beginning

In the beginning was the word, and the word was "bugger." Not a particularly auspicious word for a universe to start on, on the whole, but since Alf had just dropped his hammer on his foot, Reg supposed it could have been a lot worse.

"Look," Reg said, "could you try being a bit more careful? At least until I've got the controls wired up properly."

"Careful? You're not the one who has just had to keep his finger on a galaxy for three hours while the glue set." Alf retrieved his hammer from the shed floor, putting it back on the rack of tools. Thanks to their profession, it was quite a big rack of tools, and some of the items on it probably didn't feature in many other sheds—not even the ones of the people who built model airplanes. "I'm always careful."

"Really?" Reg adjusted his flat cap in a pointed manner. It was quite a hard object to adjust pointedly, but after working with Alf for a while, Reg had acquired the knack. "So it wasn't you who left a big un-welded spot on the job we did for the Ice Giants, letting a bunch of random Norwegians in?"

"No one ever proved that was where they came from," Alf shot back, "so it wasn't like we were liable, or anything. Anyway, I'll have the dog in to get rid of them eventually. Now hand me that 3/8 wrench, would you? I've got a nebula here that still needs to be bolted in."

Some people, Reg had heard, some nice, sensible people, who didn't like having to muck about with conversion tables every time they wanted to get the right size of bearing for a galaxy, made their universes in metric—not much chance of that here, though.

Reg was nominally younger than Alf, but time and space were always a bit complicated inside the shed. So it could be hard to tell, some days. However, Mrs. Reg sometimes suggested that had less to do with messing about with the space/time thingy than it had to do with the effects of sheds generally, which always, she reckoned, had the effect of stopping those within from ever growing up properly.

Reg put that thought from his mind and handed over the wrench. Alf accepted it with the kind of grunt that Alf was wont to fall into as a means of communication when he was concentrating. He then made a couple of minute adjustments to the universe, which was currently balancing precariously on the edge of the workbench—well, minute on this side, anyway.

"Now then," Alf muttered, "come and give me a hand with this bit. Careful now, it's a bit-"

"Hi, there!"

Reg had the presence of mind to catch the universe as Alf knocked it off the bench, lifting it carefully back into place before turning to look at the newcomer.

The newcomer turned out to be a girl. Even with her wearing a boiler suit, it was quite impossible to be mistaken on that point. She appeared to be about eighteen. Her hair was blonde and tied back very precisely to keep it away from features that would have made most artists give up when they couldn't capture their beauty—or at least suggest that their owner might want to go out for a drink with them.

"Hi!" the girl said. "I'm Cindy."

Just that. Not, 'I'm Cindy, and I'm here to make you drop things,' or, 'I'm Cindy, and I'm here to model boiler suits and make you wish you were somewhere between twenty and a thousand years younger.' She only said her name, like Reg and Alf were somehow supposed to know what she was there for.

Unfortunately, it then occurred to Reg that he did.

He'd had a talk with Mrs. Reg about it last night, in fact—at least if you could call him making occasional noises about it as he tried to read the paper "a talk." She'd said something about her sister's kid needing something to do for work experience, and how it might be nice to get someone involved in the trade, what with Reg not getting any younger, except on those days when Alf dropped the jars they kept the time in before they could be properly decanted.

Which meant that now, Reg was faced with a choice. He could try suggesting to Alf that they should take on some chit of a girl right when they were in the middle of a big order from the whole "parallel worlds" contingent, or he could try explaining to Mrs. Reg why he hadn't. As a man who could recognize the lesser of two evils as easily as he could recognize a Phillips-head screwdriver, there was only one thing for it.

"Hello, Cindy. We've been waiting for you to show up."

"So… when do I get to help out with the universes?" Cindy asked, making Reg wince. She'd been with them in the shed for half a day now. It had been quite a busy half-day, given that Reg had had to come up with plenty of things to keep the girl away from anything important—not to mention away from Alf, who was grumpy enough about having people in his shed, even when he wasn't trying to work out the ratios for planetary distribution.

Thankfully, Alf had made things a bit easier by knocking off early, saying something about his back acting up, but all that really meant was that Reg was stuck in a seemingly increasingly-tiny shed with his wife's bored niece.

"I'll tell you what, why don't you go and put the kettle on?"

"But you've had like five cups of tea already. And anyway, I'm here to learn stuff, not to make stupid tea."

"Ah," Reg said, in a suitably wise tone he had copied from Alec Guinness in *Star Wars*, "but you see, you can't hope to make a universe properly until you have mastered the perfect cuppa. If you can't get the balance of milk to tea just right, how can you hope to blend nebulae? If you can't strain out the leaves, what are you going to do with asteroids? And without knowing the secret of the second lump of sugar…" Reg struggled to think what the second lump of sugar could be a metaphor for. "Well, it just isn't going to work, is it?"

"Oh, all right. I'll make your stupid tea."

Cindy stomped off to the corner of the shed where they kept an ancient kettle, managing to convey merely by the tone of her footsteps that her aunt would be hearing all about this. That was a thought to make even Reg cringe.

"Look," he said. "How about if I give you a go at something straightforward, like slotting a few planets into place? It really needs thinner fingers than mine anyway."

"Oh, can I, Uncle Reg?"

Reg shrugged. "I don't see why not. You've got to be careful, mind. Now, you'll need-"

"The tweezers, the smallest Allen key, and the spot welder," Cindy said. "I know. I've been reading up on this for *ages*."

"You have?"

"Of course. Why do you think I wanted to come here? I thought Aunty Vera *told* you that I wanted to go into creating when I left school."

"Well..."

"Only for one of the big companies, obviously."

Reg tried not to let that get to him. After all, it was all about the big names these days: General Operating Division, Shiva's Creation and Destruction (Ltd), Microsoft, etc. It was hardly surprising that the girl didn't see the virtues of the small businessman doing what he loved. He'd just have to show her that a universe that didn't come pre-loaded with Windows was something to be cherished.

So he spent the next twenty minutes trying to convey pearls of wisdom as his niece teased planets into the goldilocks zone around stars and then spot welded them before they could wander off. There were a couple of teething troubles, but what was wrong with a couple of extra near orbit planets, anyway. The girl had talent, and it was obvious. She even seemed to have mastered double-retrospinning, which Reg had to admit that he'd never gotten the hang of, preferring Alf's method of whacking a damn great blob of blu-tack on one side instead.

It was going so well that he hardly thought twice about leaving her to it when the phone rang. It was Mrs. Reg, checking up on how things were going. Reg assured her, "Yes, everything is fine… no, really love… no, I won't be late home for dinner, not if it is going to be steak and kidney…" before putting the phone back and turning round again.

Things had changed quite a lot in the course of a minute and a half, like Cindy's expression, for one thing. It had gone from a look of self-possessed confidence to something more usually associated with people who had just received an unexpected tax demand. Then, there was the universe. It seemed to have broken free of its strapping, and it was now whirling freely.

"Cindy?"

"Um…"

"What did you do?!"

"I didn't do anything," the girl insisted. "Well, nothing I shouldn't have, anyway. I just thought that, since we'd need to be sure of the orbits of the planets, we'd need to get it running for a quick test, and-"

"You *set it running*?!" Reg demanded.

"There's no need to shout."

"'No need to shout,' she says. She sets a universe running without any of the safeties on *and* with the randomness generator still engaged, and she says, 'There's no need to shout.'" Reg took off his flat cap, holding it in both hands like some kind of shield. "Do you have any idea of what might happen?"

"Um..."

"No, didn't think so. Neither do I. That's the randomness generator for you. I mean, I know Alf likes everything handcrafted, down to the last little moon. Personally, I think life's too short, so I tend to leave it running in the background, like the radio—only the radio isn't about to fill the place with... well, whatever it feels like, now, is it?!"

"Oh." Cindy looked momentarily distraught, and then very determined. "Well, we'll just have to do something about it, then. Presumably there's a cutoff switch in here somewhere-"

Thankfully, Reg could still move reasonably quickly when he wanted to. He grabbed Cindy's hand before it had more than brushed the thing, and he managed to pull her away quickly enough that she only lost a couple of layers of skin.

"Ow! That *really* hurt!"

"What do you expect if you stick your fingers into a wall of space/time moving at several light years a second?" Reg barked. "I thought you'd know that the emergency controls for these things are always kept outside, for precisely that reason."

"There are emergency controls?" Cindy asked. "Well, then, all we need to do is-"

"Those would be the emergency controls I was just going to finish wiring up when you arrived," Reg said. "So that's out."

"Well-"

"...likewise are trying to get in through random gaps in the surface—because I do a better welding job than that, even if Alf doesn't—trying to cut the power, and hitting it with any kind of blunt object."

Cindy looked at the rotating universe for several seconds. "Oh. Sorry. Um... so is there anything we *can* do?"

"Stay and watch, mostly," Reg said. "If we're very, *very* lucky, something useful will come up. With the randomness generator on, you never know."

"And if it doesn't?"

"Then I reckon you can be the one to explain to Alf why three weeks' worth of work is down the drain."

Cindy looked a little pensive. "Um... I hope something comes up."

Reg nodded, mostly because he knew that regardless of whoever would be explaining things to Alf, *he* would be the one explaining them to Mrs. Reg. "Me too."

Fifteen Percent

Light and Dark sat under the red half sky, looking out over the flat empty spaces of the world they had been given to play with, and they sang. Light sang the way she looked, with pure beauty and elegance—her tones floating over the unborn world's air. Rivers and streams sprang up in response to her call, dividing up the empty landscape.

Dark was squatter and more heavily built. His singing was rhythmical, pulsing with a heartbeat slower than time. He sang up mountains, rising between the rivers; and he sang up plains and rocks.

Where their voices met, they harmonized, until even they couldn't tell which note was which; and green things grew, rising out of the ground in a way that would have had most allotment owners breaking their trowels over their knees in jealousy.

They sang as the first clouds touched the sky. They sang as rain fell, softly at first, but then with an intensity that said it had heard of Wales and was determined to get into the big leagues. It rained until-

"Excuse me. I say, *excuse me!*"

Light and Dark stopped singing for a moment—the forces of creation roiling around them. They looked at one another and then at the man who was walking towards them. He had a briefcase in one hand and a piece of paper in the other.

"Did you sing that up?" Light asked.

Dark shrugged. "I thought you did. We could sing it away."

But by then, the creature was close, and they were meant to be singing things up, in any case, not getting rid of them. So they let it approach. It looked a little like Dark, in that it was male, though it was skinnier and older and wore a strange kind of clothing that seemed to be woven from spun fibers made from oil, rather than from sensible firmament—the way their clothes were.

"Alvis Moon," the creature said, extending a hand. Light and Dark stared at it. "That's my name," it explained.

"Light."

"Dark."

"Great, great. Listen, I heard you both singing just now. It was… wow!"

Light shrugged. Singing was singing. How else were you meant to make things?

"And I was thinking," the strange creature said, "that you could really go far. You know, with the right management."

"Far?" Dark asked. "Why would we go far? We need to sing here."

"I mean," the man replied, "that your talents aren't getting the audience they deserve, and I could do something about that, if you let me."

"But it is not about an audience," Light pointed out. "It is about making the world."

"Ah, a real pair of artists, I see."

Dark shook his head. "No, we sing. We do not paint."

Alvis Moon did not sigh. Light got the impression that he very *carefully* did not sigh.

"Look, let's stop kidding around, all right? I could make you both stars."

Light considered that. She had always liked stars. They were bright, like her, and if you got close enough to them, they could keep you warm. When Dark was busy running things, she liked to look at them. She thought that she might quite like to be one of them, for a while.

"Could we, Dark?"

"We have to finish this world," Dark said. "It is our sacred trust."

"Hey, I'm not in the business of getting in the way of a man's sacred trust," Alvis explained. "Of course you'd have to finish this gig. Only, with me in tow, you might actually get paid properly. I mean, what are you getting for it now?"

"We are getting the joy of creation," Dark said. "We are getting the world, just as we want it, and all the things in it made with our song in their hearts."

"Is that all?" Alvis asked.

Dark shrugged. "It is what there is."

The strange man reached up to put an arm around Dark's shoulders. It took some doing. "Buddy, are you going to be glad you met me."

"I don't know," Dark said. "Am I?"

"Yes. Yes, you are," Alvis assured him.

Dark stormed into Light's dressing room. "I am *not* glad that I met Alvis Moon," he declared.

"Dark, I'm trying to get dressed. We're on stage in half an hour."

The last few weeks had been busy ones. Light hadn't become a star yet, but she had learned what it meant. She had learned the meaning of a lot of words, including "worldwide tour", "giving the audience what they want", and "fifteen percent of everything". Alvis had been quite adamant that she should learn the meaning of the last one.

"Why would you want to get dressed?" Dark demanded.

"What do you mean? I can't go on stage naked."

"But you could sing yourself clothes. Why put on human… things?"

Light picked up the dress she was due to wear tonight. "But this is sparklier. And it's by Dior… or so Alvis told me. Whoever that is, he sings nice dresses."

"I think the dresses you sang for yourself were nicer," Dark commented.

"The audience seems to like them."

"And why do you care what humans think?" Dark paced the dressing room. "This is wrong, Light. This is not what we are for."

Light put on her dress, surveying herself in it. It shone. "We're singing, aren't we?"

"In theaters. Which we do not even sing up first."

"There's nothing wrong with that," Light said. She quite liked standing there without a sudden mountain range interrupting proceedings. She quite liked the way people seemed to enjoy her singing.

"There is *everything* wrong with that," Dark insisted, and the rumble of his voice made the building shake. "He wants me to sing something called *Swannee River* tonight, but there will be no river. How can that be right?"

Light shrugged. "It's entertainment, Dark."

"But it is not about entertainment," Dark insisted. "It is about making a world."

Light waved a hand vaguely. "Oh, Alvis says that anyone can make a world, but not everyone can make people feel something."

Dark thought for a minute. "Yes, they can. Logically, just by existing in proximity to other people-"

"That's not what I mean. You know what?"

"It is a word. One that-"

"I think that you're jealous."

Dark stared at her. "Jealous?"

Light nodded. "You're jealous that people like me more than you. You're jealous that I'm the one who gets the attention, but you don't see how hard I have to work at it. I won't let myself feel bad just because you want me to, you know."

Dark's brow furrowed. "I do not feel jealous."

"Of course you do. Well, I'm sorry, but things just are the way they are."

"Yes," Dark agreed. "Otherwise, they would be a different way."

Light pouted. "Oh, why are you so… so *stupid*?"

"I am not stupid."

"Alvis isn't stupid. He understands me. He…" Light remembered the words eventually, "respects my artistic integrity."

"I am *not stupid*!" A small tree burst up through the floor as Dark said it, then he turned for the door. "I am leaving. We still have a job to do, and I am going to do it. Will you come with me?"

Light looked at the tree and sniffed. "Not if you're going to go around being such a bully about things. And trashing dressing rooms? No. I'm staying here."

She waited until Dark was gone before she let herself cry. Where the tears fell, flowers grew up. By the time Alvis came in to find out why she wasn't on stage, she could have started her own flower shop.

"What's going on?" he demanded. "Why aren't you out there singing?"

Light sniffled. "It's Dark," she said. "He's gone."

"Gone? He can't be gone. We had a contract."

"He's gone," Light insisted. "I don't know what to do."

She started to cry again. Eventually, Alvis put an arm around her shoulders, looking quite uncomfortable about it. "What you have to remember," he said, "is that even the great bands break up eventually. Creative differences, and so forth."

"You mean the way that he wanted to create valleys and rocks and things?"

"...while you focus on your art. Exactly. Although, right now, I'd like you to focus on getting out on stage. We've got twenty thousand people who've paid for tickets, you know."

Something Dark had said came back to her. "Dark thinks that we should be focusing on completing the original job. We *are* going to complete the world, aren't we?"

"Sure, sure," Alvis said. "Right after we release the greatest hits album."

"But *how* are we going to complete the world? I mean, Dark is gone."

"Well, we'll see about that too," Alvis said. "Does he not know what a contract guaranteeing me total options over all creative rights means?"

"Probably not," Light said. "*I* don't know what that means."

Alvis sighed. "It means that I get to say where and when he sings, and for how much. It means he does the job I tell him to do. And if he doesn't, well, I'll just get in some session musicians to help finish this gig."

"Session musicians?" Light asked.

"Sure. How do you feel about the Nashville sound?"

"I don't know what that is either," Light admitted. She thought for a second. "Do you have this total control stuff with me too?"

Alvis shrugged. "Well, sure. I wouldn't be much of an A&R guy without it, would I?"

"I don't think I like that," Light said.

"Sorry, kid. That's show business. Now, are you going to get out onto that stage, or am I going to have to sue you for breach of contract?"

"I don't think I'd like that either," Light said.

"Then get out there and sing."

Light nodded. "I'll sing."

She sang. As she sang, Alvis Moon floated up, glowing brighter as he did it—past the ceiling, past the clouds, past the sky…

Light kept singing until he hung there, and grew, and changed, shining exactly fifteen percent of her brightness down on the world. When she was sure that he was well and truly stuck there, she set off after Dark, but she did stop to finish the concert first.

Light eventually found Dark and they finished what they started, although they subsequently decided that solo careers would suit them best. In his new form, Alvis Moon continued to flit between them, presumably in the hopes of eventually getting back payments on his share of the royalties.

Extinct

"It's alive, Doctor Franks. It's *alive!*"

I'm starting to think that the new assistant I've hired for the lab isn't going to work out. I'd like to think that I'm not a harsh man, as employers go, but there are limits. It's not that Gilbert doesn't do good work, as such, but he insists on saying things like that. Some of his working practices are, frankly, odd—like that thing he has about installing big levers everywhere and throwing them at random moments. It's not really the sort of thing I should be encouraging, as a serious research scientist. Still, I try to keep my cool. My fiancé Beth is always telling me that I need to learn to relax more.

"Of course it's alive, Gilbert," I point out. "We're working in the field of advanced genetics. Practically everything we do is alive. Now concentrate, please. We have to get that job for the Australians finished by the end of the week."

"The Tasmanian devils?" Gilbert says, rebuttoning his waistcoat. Why he's wearing a waistcoat, I don't know, but for some reason, he always insists on dressing more like a Victorian gentleman than a proper grad-student—which is to say, like something that has thrown on a white coat after arriving from a homeless shelter. "I finished those yesterday."

"It was meant to be thylacines, not Tasmanian devils," I point out, "for the simple reason that one of those is extinct, and the other isn't." I sigh. "Presumably, we'll have to start again then?"

"Oh." Gilbert bites his lip. "Well, maybe that's for the best. The ones I made kind of… got loose, and now they're just spinning round and round in the basement."

"That's not what Tasmanian devils do, Gilbert."

"Tell it to these ones, Doctor. Actually, don't try to tell them anything. I can't understand a word they say."

I've had enough. "Gilbert, we're trying to bring back valuable elements of the world's natural history here. Please, try to take it seriously."

"Sorry, Doctor Franks."

The difficulty with the project, of course, is trying to balance everything. People don't seem to *want* every animal back, for some reason, and we only get licenses to create some things. That means trying to think about the kind of checks and balances that need to occur in a complex ecosystem without recreating the whole thing. Take the time we brought back the Brontosaurus. No one wanted T-Rexes either, which meant that we were practically overrun with the thing before someone pointed out that in sufficient numbers, the Falkland Islands Wolf might be persuaded to view them as a buffet. I find that a ratio of approximately a thousand wolves per dinosaur works quite well.

Suffice it to say that this is a *highly* responsible job—not one for a man who can't keep his cool. The paperwork alone would be enough to drive a man quite mad if he weren't careful. And as for the dodo, with its refusal to stay resurrected for more than five minutes without being eaten… well, let's just say that some projects are easier than others, shall we?

A crash from the back of the lab tells me that Gilbert is working again. I'm going to have to let him go. I know it. It isn't just his unfortunate tendency to raise lightning rods when I'm trying to do some serious work around here. It's the way he insists on treating everything like it's somehow fun. Real science isn't fun.

"Doctor Franks," Gilbert hollers from the back. "I think I may have a solution to the dodo issue."

I sigh. "Does it involve grafting on fragments of sabre tooth tiger DNA so that we suddenly have a small flightless bird with the instinct to jump on gazelles and bring them down with a single bite?"

"You got my note then?"

I retreat to my office. That just isn't how science works. It really isn't fun. Science is about method, and procedure, repetition and the sensible accumulation of results, which means it's also mainly funding applications. Tell me how someone is meant to find the fun in those.

Talking of which, there are a couple of important letters from the funding bodies sitting on my desk when I get back. The university's internal mail must have dropped them off, in those ineffable ways it always does. I open them and scan the contents, checking that all the applications I put in have been nicely… oh.

Dr. Franks, the first one reads, *We regret to inform you that your application for funding has been rejected. The association feels that there are ethical issues surrounding your work with which it cannot associate itself. Yours, etc.*

The second one isn't any better, though it goes more for the "*these straightened financial times*" angle. It's like they can't see the importance of my work. My great, great work. Ahem. Well, I'm sure we'll just have to muddle through. Just because things have gone a little wrong, that does not mean I'm suddenly going to start gibbering, or doing anything dangerously insane.

"Dr. Franks?"

I sigh. "What is it, Gilbert? If you want to start up 'bring your brain to work in a jar' day again, the answer is still no."

"It's nothing like that, Doctor. Although now you mention it... could I-"

"No." Like I said, one little funding blip will not make me stray from the path of true science.

"Oh. Well, the dean is on line one."

The dean is eager to talk to me, apparently. He's also eager to assure me that the decision to amalgamate my department with the School of Fungus had nothing to do with him, and that it is emphatically not down to the way I do Frankenstein science. I point out to him that I *don't* do Frankenstein science, and he says that's why it can't be down to it.

Damn it. It's almost like the universe is trying to tell me something. But, no, I will not give in to that kind of superstitious nonsense. I will not—not even if it's the elephant in the room.

Instead, I get to work on some DNA sequencing for our Woolly Mammoth project.

By half past five, I've done so much that I'm sure we could reconstruct an entire trunk if we chose to. It's not a patch on the dodos, but at least that means it might stay alive a while.

The door to the lab opens, admitting Beth and also a young man, whose arm she seems to be clinging onto in a way I'm sure fiancés shouldn't, especially when the arm in question is not that of an impending husband. For some reason, the image of an arm picked up from a pile of spares and sewn onto something springs to mind. I ignore it.

"Beth, darling? What are you doing here?"

Beth glances away. "Hugo, I… I'm sorry, but I seem to see so little of you these days."

"Well, I've been so busy on the… hang on, what are you saying, darling?"

"She's saying she doesn't need you and your crazy science anymore," the young man says, *not very helpfully*, I think. I look to Beth.

"Hugo," Beth says, "I'm breaking off the engagement. Steven here is… well, you just know sometimes, don't you? It's like the universe is sending you a message about what you're meant to do with your life or something. I know you don't believe that, but it's true. I'm sorry."

She walks out, leaving me to sit down on the edge of a bench hard enough that I knock over two retorts. Squid and rice plant DNA starts to combine, and I idly consider the possibilities of a one-stop source of a nice seafood dinner, just before Gilbert comes along to sweep it up.

"Gilbert," I ask. "Are you happy?"

"Oh, yes, Dr. Franks. I have my job, and my wife… well, most of her, and my collection of thumbs. I'm about as happy as a chap can be, really."

I sit there a little longer, and then I look up at the ceiling. *All right, all right,* I think, *in the general direction of everything. I can take a hint. And at least there's one thing it can help with.*

"Gilbert?"

"Yes, Doctor?"

"Get the dodo jars out again—plus those thylacine ones from before… and the shark ones. Oh, and put up some more lightning rods in here. We'll show them who isn't up to this!"

I pause. It occurs to me there's something I ought to do.

"Haha. Haha. Hahahaha!"

There. Much better.

Inspiration

It started with the inevitable question—the one that had become a joke between them because of its sheer awfulness, the one Rebecca asked Peter every time they met up to trade drinks and short stories, the way they had when they had been at university and when half the English department had joined in. She'd first asked him the question back when she'd been a struggling young writer, because she hadn't known any better, because Peter had managed to have books published, and because he even *looked* like a writer with his long dark hair and even longer leather coat.

"Go on, then. Where do you get your ideas?"

Maybe if anyone else had asked it that first time, Peter would have laughed at them, or snubbed them, or something. But Rebecca… well, she'd always been the one the boys went after, with the kind of cheerleader good looks she tried her best to mute, and Peter had been no exception—not that they'd gone that far, in the end.

So Peter made up an answer. And he kept making up answers. It became a game. Every time Rebecca asked, which was every time they met up, he had a new one for her. He got them from big books full of ideas, he'd say, or he swapped them with other authors at garage sales. Even after they'd left university, even after Peter had become better known and everyone else had drifted off to do the kinds of things people did after university, Rebecca had kept asking it.

Tonight, though, Rebecca wasn't sure if she should. Peter seemed kind of down, nursing a drink even before she arrived. She'd heard something about him being under pressure from his publishers to deliver more often, and he'd told her about Sandy running off with another guy who didn't spend so much time in worlds of his own invention that he forgot about her, so maybe that was it.

"Hey," she said, ordering a drink of her own. They'd long since established that even though Rebecca worked in admin and pulled in a fraction of what Peter did, she was going to buy her own drinks. "You going to tell me what's wrong?"

Peter shrugged. "Do you ever get the feeling that you're leaching the people around you dry? That you're just a parasite?"

"Not often."

"Well, I do. The publishers come running, and every time, *every* time, I… no, I didn't come here for that. I came here to see you." He smiled, and it was obvious that it was forced, but Rebecca was willing to go along with it. "Did you get the beginnings of the one I'm working on at the moment?"

"Sure," Rebecca said. "Amazing as usual."

"You say that, but I can never be sure these days."

"It's better than the one I sent you, I bet."

Peter shrugged. "You say that, but I think it's more that you don't put your stories out there."

"And I don't have your ideas," Rebecca said. "It's the ideas that make it, Peter. That thing with the Bishop and the house of cards? Brilliant."

"I'm glad you think so," Peter said, although he didn't sound very glad.

Rebecca decided to cheer him up a little by giving into the inevitable. No doubt, he would have something good. "So, where *do* you get your ideas?"

Peter was quiet for a few seconds, which was odd. Normally, he had something worked out right away. That was half the fun. Tonight, though, he sat and stared at her, sipping his coffee. At last, he cocked his head to one side. "Would you like to see?"

It was a shop. They had driven for almost fifteen minutes, into the most old-fashioned part of the city, where you could still find strange little shops that looked like they might not have changed in a hundred years—possibly including the owner, in many cases. The sign on the front said *J. Hibbert & Co Inspirations*. Rebecca looked up at it and laughed.

"Oh, very funny," she said. "What? You saw the sign and decided to make it the punch line for the question?"

Peter shook his head. "I'm not joking."

"Of course you're joking. 'I get my inspiration from this little shop' is one of the classics."

"There's a reason for that," Peter said, and he stepped inside.

Rebecca hesitated for a second or two. A joke was a joke, but Peter seemed to be taking things a bit far. Still, maybe she should play along for now. It could be fun, and it looked like Peter could do with a bit of fun. He seemed very tense tonight. Deciding to get into the spirit of things, she followed Peter into the shop.

Inside, it was even more old fashioned than from the outside. There was a big oak counter, with a set of pigeon holes up on the wall just behind it, making the place look a little like the reception area of a particularly strange hotel—strange because of all the other things taking up space there. There was a clutter of objects, or possibly even objects d'art, ranging from a couple of knobby statues to some kind of ceremonial sword.

Behind the desk, there was a man. He was not a tall man, meaning that Rebecca could look down and see the perfectly circular bald patch, like a monk's tonsure, on top of his head. He wore an almost eye-wateringly patterned waistcoat over relatively plain shirt and pants. He could have been any age from about fifty upwards.

"Ah, Peter, you've come," the man welcomed. "I was beginning to think that you might not keep your appointment."

"Appointment?" Rebecca questioned. "So this isn't just some random shop Peter has picked out because he liked the sign?"

Peter looked at her, then over at the man. "Joshua, I'm sorry. Rebecca here doesn't believe me. Could you perhaps tell her what it is that you do here? Just the basics, obviously."

"Obviously," Joshua, who was presumably the J. Hibbert of recent signage fame, said. "Well, there isn't much to say, really. I provide a valuable service for authors and artists of all descriptions, by supplying small moments of inspiration to meet their needs."

Rebecca blinked a few times. "Is this a joke? I mean, Peter didn't put you up to this, did he?"

"Oh, no, I wouldn't have time for anything like that," Joshua said, "and besides, I believe jokes have rather more in the way of chickens crossing roads and so forth. One of our more enduring efforts, I've always felt."

Rebecca looked over to Peter, but he still appeared deadly serious.

"You actually mean it, don't you?" she asked. "So how does it work? People come in here, and they see that clutter and get inspired? Or do you keep fragments of things written down in those pigeon holes to give to people?"

Joshua smiled. "Very good. That is indeed how my ancestor, the late James Hibbert, began this shop. More recently, however, which is to say, in the last hundred and fifty years or so, things have… moved on a little." He looked to Peter. "I take it that the young lady is here to see how we do things?"

Peter hesitated just a fraction before he nodded.

"Very well then. I have the time." He pressed something on the underside of his desk, and a door behind him swung open, revealing a set of stairs leading down. "Perhaps you would like to take the tour?"

Rebecca was generally a lot more sensible than to take tours of random basements with strange men. But Peter was there, and she had to admit that she was intrigued. Maybe there would even be something down there that would help her with her own work.

"Okay," she said. "Why not?"

Joshua Hibbert nodded. "Why not indeed."

The tour took a little longer than Rebecca had anticipated, mostly because she had not anticipated more than a single basement room. The shop, however, appeared to extend for several basements' worth of rooms, connected by the kind of corridors and unexpected pipe work normally only found in thrillers, at that point where the hero needs somewhere to shoot that will give off nice gouts of steam.

So far, Joshua had shown her the store rooms where he kept old boxes full of things to inspire potential authors; a large mechanical machine, apparently copied from Charles Babbage back in the nineteenth century, designed to generate random idea combinations; and a small network of tunnels that he claimed were home to wild ideas roaming freely, doing strange things to reality—although Rebecca suspected he might have been joking about that. Admittedly, Peter didn't laugh at it, but he had to be joking.

"And now," Joshua said, "the piece de resistance, as the French almost never say."

It was a room—a circular room about twenty feet across, to be precise—with what appeared to be an old-fashioned barber's chair in the middle. A steel helmet hung above it, held in place by a swivel arm. Around the walls were nine evenly spaced hatches, covered by steel grills. Wires led from each one to the chair. There was also a large lever not far from it too.

"What's this?" Rebecca asked, because it wasn't the sort of set up where you could do anything else.

Peter put a hand on her shoulder, but he spoke to Joshua. "Perhaps if we do me first, she'll understand."

Joshua looked from him to the chair. "Very well, if you think it best."

"I do."

Peter went over to sit in the chair. There were restraints on it that fastened across his wrists, ankles, and chest, but Peter didn't seem to mind.

"They are for his safety," Joshua explained. "I have done away with the inefficient methods preferred by my forefathers when it comes to inspiration, preferring instead to generate it directly from the source and transfer it straight into the waiting individual. This device does that, but the process can produce some muscular spasming that must be guarded against to avoid even the slightest chance of injury."

He moved over to lower the helmet down onto Peter's head, and Rebecca found herself wondering why she was watching while he did it. This seemed odd, even insane, yet she wasn't doing anything to stop it. Maybe it was the fact that Peter didn't seem to mind. If anything, he seemed to welcome it. He seemed almost… hungry for it.

Once the helmet was in place, Joshua moved over to the large lever. Rebecca moved to stand beside him.

"Are we all set?" Joshua asked, but he didn't wait for an answer. He just threw the lever. Sparks leaped from the helmet, and the metal grills around the room rolled up, revealing glass cases. In those glass cases were women, though no women Rebecca had ever seen before had glowed with a light so bright that it was hard to look at them.

"What *is* this?" Rebecca demanded. "Who are they? Why are they in there?"

She could think of a dozen potential explanations; none of them were nice. What had Peter gotten her into?

"Those are muses," Joshua said, "and as for what they're doing here…"

Light leapt from one of the cases and along the wires, leading to the chair. For several seconds, the steel helmet glowed, while Peter's form went rigid. If he hadn't been so eager to climb into the chair, Rebecca would have sworn he was being electrocuted. Finally, it faded, and Joshua moved over to undo the arrangement holding him in place.

Peter practically leapt up, and his expression was entirely changed from earlier. "I can see it! I can see what I have to write!"

"Always happy to be of service," Joshua said.

"But not all of it," Peter complained. "There's not enough."

The smaller man shrugged. "Perhaps later, after your friend has had a turn?"

Rebecca started at that. "What, you really think that I'm going to get into that chair?"

Peter turned to her. "It works, Rebecca. It works so well. I can see the ideas going around in my head perfectly. I know you always wanted to be a writer. Well, this is how."

"I'm fairly sure it isn't," Rebecca shot back. "And what about those women? What are you two doing to them here?"

"Those aren't women," Peter insisted. "Those are muses."

"Peter is right," Joshua said. "They are mythological beings that merely choose to take human form. They have long inspired artists of all kinds. It is what they do. I have merely made the system more… efficient."

"By locking them up?" Rebecca demanded. "You're mad, both of you. You're locking up people, thinking that they're these non-existent creatures, and then you're messing about with some machine that's just… well, crazy, and-"

"Just try it," Peter suggested. "You know I would never do anything to hurt you, Rebecca. I'm trying to help you. This is your chance—your *only* chance. Or do you think that you're going to make it on your own? You haven't so far."

He knew where to hit so that it hurt, Rebecca had to admit. The idea that she could just sit down in some magical machine and it would give her a career like Peter's was tempting—too tempting. But Rebecca could be stronger than that. She shook her head.

"No, Peter. I'm not doing it. Now let those poor women go, or I'll call the cops."

"No," Peter said, "you won't."

He moved quickly, and he was stronger than he looked. Between him and Joshua, it took less than a minute to get her strapped down in the machine.

"I was hoping you would climb in," Peter said. "It's so much easier when they climb in. You could have not known what was happening." He looked to Joshua. "She'll be enough?"

"Oh, I should think so." The little man lowered the helmet carefully over Rebecca's head. "You'll get enough to finish that novel of yours, just like the others."

"Good," Peter's voice wavered, and for a moment, Rebecca thought that he would stop whatever was happening. "I… I'll be upstairs."

He turned and walked away.

"Now that he's gone, I should probably explain," Joshua said. "Muses are such difficult creatures, and they need feeding. Specifically, they need feeding with human experiences. Memories, if you will. Thankfully, my machine works both ways."

"You're going to-"

"Not me. The muses. Don't worry though, this won't hurt a bit; or at least, you won't remember if it does. None of Peter's other friends did. You know, of all my clients, he is easily the most regular."

For a moment, Rebecca found herself thinking of some of their other friends. The ones who had drifted off, given up on the writer's life. How many of them had come to this place with Peter? What kind of state had they left it in? She found herself thinking of their faces.

Then Joshua threw the lever the opposite way to the one he had thrown it for Peter. The glass grills slid open again, revealing nine very hungry looking women, and Rebecca started to dream…

She dreamed that she was back at home as a little girl, with all the family pets she had ever owned. She dreamed that she was at university, and she had just met Peter. She dreamed that he had suggested they go back to his place, and she had said no, because that was what all the boys wanted from her and, anyway, she had an exam in the morning.

Then she dreamed that she was in a place with a marble floor, sitting on a white stone couch, beside a woman who looked faintly familiar. They were both wearing long dresses that had gone out of fashion a couple of thousand years before. The woman beside her had flowing dark hair, and her features were so beautiful they almost hurt to look at.

"You did not get into the chair willingly," she remarked. "Why not? They always do normally."

The chair? What chair? It took Rebecca an effort to remember. When she did, she remembered that the last time she had seen the woman beside her, she had been in a small glass case. "I didn't want anything to do with it. It felt wrong."

"But to get what you wanted…"

"It wouldn't have been me," Rebecca said. "Besides, I only kept seeing Peter because… well, I thought he was my friend."

"Hmm… yes. I think we can work with that. But we must move quickly. I am Calliope. My sisters and I are hungry—always so hungry. But for this, we can hold back."

She reached out, and her hands touched Rebecca's forehead.

Rebecca was back in the chair. She was there, and she could feel the gaps in her where memories had been. There was nothing flowing from her at the moment, and in the spaces where her memories had been, there was something new. Inspiration burned in her the way it must have in the hearts of the great composers, or the great poets, or indeed, the great escapologists.

She twisted in the straps that held her in a way that would never have occurred to her before. It was so obvious now that she could see it, but before it had simply seemed out of reach. She turned her arm just so, and in an instant, it was free enough to unbuckle other straps. In a matter of seconds, she was out of the chair, and the steel helmet was in her hands as she tore it from the frame.

Joshua stood there staring at her. He was not a big man, but he was still big enough that Rebecca did not want to have to fight him. Instead, she threw the metal helmet at him. It missed as he ducked, smashing into the glass holding one of the muses, which cracked. As Joshua spun, a look of anguish on his features, Rebecca shoved him aside and ran. She did not run for the stairs though. That would have meant too many dangers. Instead, she ran deeper into the basement, into the space Joshua had claimed was full of wild ideas.

Rebecca could hear him somewhere behind her, not running, just walking and talking as he went.

"This is really very foolish," he said. "Why delay something so inevitable? Come back now, and we will say no more about it. It isn't like you will die, after all. You simply won't remember. And let's face it, you probably weren't doing much with your life anyway."

Rebecca ignored that. She just kept going down the corridors, which glowed redly with the light of unused thoughts.

"Or maybe you're thinking you can lose me here?" Joshua said. "Here where there are so many ideas. I'm sorry to say it doesn't work like that. A sufficiently-focused mind can use them, you see. For example…"

The next corner Rebecca turned revealed a dead end. She swore and turned, just in time to find Joshua bearing down on her. She didn't panic. Instead, she smiled. "So all I have to do is focus?"

"You're planning to fight me with ideas? You wouldn't know where to start." Joshua laughed. Mid laugh, he waved a hand vaguely. Rebecca found that she was no longer in a corridor, but at the bottom of a deep pit, with the shop owner looking down at her and sun streaming in behind him. "It's something of a classic, don't you think?"

"Hackneyed," Rebecca countered, but that was probably a good thing. It meant, for example, that when she thought *and with a spring she was free,* she actually did spring right out of the hole. That was what you got for using ideas straight out of pulp fiction.

"You'll regret that," Joshua promised, and conjured a tribe of blowgun wielding jungle natives from nowhere. Rebecca thought again, and they stopped to ask her for directions, having turned out to be a bunch of marketing executives on their way to a costume party.

That seemed to be when Joshua got angry. At least, the ideas came quicker. Rebecca found herself in the middle of water, surrounded by sharks. She had them pushed away by dolphins. She found herself in a falling elevator. She arranged for it to jam, and for a conveniently handsome repairman to open the doors. Joshua tried to make him a serial killer, but by that point, Rebecca had already hit him with a wrench from his own tool belt.

"You know you cannot win," Joshua pointed out. "After all, when have you ever done anything really useful with an idea?"

"Now." Rebecca went on the attack then, imagining a sudden fall of boulders. Joshua barely jumped out of the way in time, and that just happened to put him nicely in the way of a buffalo panicked by the noise, which came running down the corridor just as soon as Rebecca could think of it. It smashed into the little man, sending him sprawling, clearly unconscious.

For a moment or two, ideas continued to roil around Rebecca, apparently unwilling to stop. They spun and they danced, demanding attention, yet every time her attention alighted on one of them, the scene in the corridor would change. It became a desert, a rolling plain, and a small tea party thrown by the Duke of Westminster in the space of about five seconds. Calmly, patiently, Rebecca walked forwards until she was just in a corridor again. Once she was sure she was alone, except for the currently sleeping form of Joshua Hibbert, she let out a long breath.

Carefully, she returned to the room with the machine in it, and she broke every pane of glass she could find, not caring that she cut her hands in the process. After that, Rebecca headed back to the shop upstairs, past the collection of things in boxes. They seemed so pointless, now that she actually looked at them. She walked out into the shop and stopped, her eyes half closed.

"Hello, Peter. I had almost forgotten you would be waiting."

"I heard the noises below. What did you do?"

Rebecca shrugged. "I ended it. No more ideas, Peter."

Peter actually looked panicked at that. "But you can't have. You can't have stopped it. No, you stupid-"

"Don't. Walk away, Peter. Do it now, and I won't even ask about all the others you've hurt."

"Walk away?" Peter looked at her like she'd just suggested that he fly to the moon. "How can I walk away? I've got a novel to finish."

"Was it like that for everyone else?" Rebecca asked. "Did each of them cost somebody?"

"They didn't die," Peter argued. "I wouldn't have done it if they'd died."

"Yes, you would have."

Peter was silent in the darkness of the shop for almost a minute. "Yes," he agreed at last, "I would've. And you know what? I'll kill you if you don't go back down there and get in that chair. I'll do it."

Rebecca nodded. "I believe you, although there isn't much point. The machine really is destroyed, Peter."

Peter shook his head and took a step forward. "Then I'll just kill you."

"No, you won't."

"You think you're going to stop me?"

Rebecca shook her head. "Not me. I'm sorry."

They came for him then. They came glowing, free, and hungry, flashing out of the dark. The muses fell on Peter in a blaze, and he fell in turn by stages—first to his knees, then to his back. They blazed brighter as they fed, until Rebecca could hardly look at them, but she forced herself to do it anyway.

When they were done, there was silence from eight of the nine, as well as from the ragged, broken thing in the leather jacket.

"We thank you for freeing us," Calliope said, with a smile that was much gentler than what she and her sisters had done. "The others feel we should reward you. Name an inspiration, and it is yours. Would you like to write a perfect novel? A great symphony? Say it, and the idea will come."

Rebecca shook her head. She stepped forward and helped Peter up from the ground. "Thanks, but no thanks." She thought back to what she had done back in the corridors. "I think I can manage on my own."

She had thought Calliope would be angry at that, but instead, her smile just widened. "Yes," the muse said, "I think you can."

Unnatural History

Nestled among the rocks, two hundred feet above base-camp, his feet wedged into the kind of cracks that would have given the average mountain goat pause for thought, Daniel checked that the fixed video camera with "BBC Un-Natural History Unit" on the side was covering the nest perfectly.

That done, he edged backwards, tried not to swear too much as the knife-edged rocks lived up to their description every time he used them for a handhold, and huddled back under his camouflage netting to wait with the other camera. He'd been waiting a while, but then, wildlife filmmaking was mostly about patience, even when it wasn't the usual sort of wildlife—well, patience and making sure that all your shots were in focus, as the idiots who kept trying to film Bigfoot without the proper lenses invariably found out. It's like they didn't know about morphic ray refraction, or something.

But, mostly, it was about patience. You could wait for weeks with nothing happening or with some stupid basilisk deciding it couldn't be bothered to turn anything into stone now that the production company had forked out for the special filters to let you film it. Then, bang! Just like that, it happened. Well, more of a crash, really, given what happened to the assistant director on that one, but the same general idea.

Take the current job, for example. A fortnight stuck halfway up a mountain, wedged under netting, watching, waiting for the phoenix to finish building its nest… and Daniel still hadn't gotten one decent shot—although, that wasn't the worst part of it. The worst part was-

"Is it here yet?"

The voice was so full of enthusiasm you could probably have siphoned it off and sold it to a country lacking in the stuff, like Belgium, without making a noticeable dent in it. It was also the kind of voice that seemed to think that a conspiratorial whisper should be loud enough to deafen anyone within three feet, just in case they didn't hear.

"Jenna, would you keep your bloody voice *down*?"

"Sorry." The intern Daniel had been lumbered with crawled into the space next to him, handing him a coffee. After two weeks, you'd have thought she'd have gotten the hang of the fact that he didn't take milk. Her face was streaked with dirt, and the makers of her all-weather clothing apparently hadn't taken mountain tops into account when they made the claim, but in spite of that, she was smiling—honestly.

"What is it, Jenna?" Daniel demanded, trying to keep his eye on the nesting site visible through the camera lens. It was as close to friendliness as he could be bothered with, by this point.

"I just wanted to see if there was anything I could do to help."

That was an obvious invitation to say, "No, go home." But he couldn't do that, apparently, as Mr. Wilks back in the offices had explained to him at some length. They had to learn some time. Besides, Daniel would need someone to help get the gear down the mountain path again.

It wasn't that he had anything particular against the girl. Well, except the whole left side of his body, given the confined space of the hide, but if there's one thing that being up a freezing mountain does for you, it's to put that kind of thought on ice. Jenna was probably perfectly nice. In fact, if Daniel had to put his finger on it, he'd say that was probably the problem. She was nice, and bright, and enthusiastic. She went "Ooh!" at things. It wasn't, as far as Daniel was concerned, how professionals behaved.

…nor was shifting so that Daniel's knee jammed into another particularly sharp rock.

"Ouch! Would you stay *still*? And stay quiet. The last thing we want is to scare the bird off. Bloody glorified chicken. Why it can't do all this somewhere convenient is beyond me."

Something about Jenna's expression told him that wasn't the sort of thing she entirely expected a leading wildlife photographer to say.

"But that's…" she began, then lowered her voice when Daniel glared at her. "How can you treat this like it's nothing?"

"I'm hardly doing that, am I?" Daniel replied. He checked to make sure there still wasn't any sign of the bird. There wasn't. "This could potentially be a behavior that no one else has filmed."

"That's not what I mean," Jenna shot back. "You're about to film a phoenix!"

Ah. Daniel was starting to understand why old Wilks had paired the girl up with him. Presumably, the old man had thought that a week or two with a real professional might knock a few of the rough edges off her—or maybe get her thrown off a mountain.

"A *phoenix*!" Jenna repeated.

Daniel shrugged, shuffling sideways so that he could look at her properly. *Was I ever that young,* he wondered. "And? If it weren't a phoenix, it'd be unicorns, or dragons, or something else. You did read what it said on the side of the cameras, didn't you?"

Jenna hesitated. "Well… yes. It says 'un-natural history unit'. What does that have to do with-"

"It means that you can't stand around going 'Wow!' every time something impossible happens, or you never get anything done."

"Oh, I'm sorry," Jenna said, in a tone that Daniel felt was slightly more sarcastic than it needed to be. "Maybe I'm just not used to the idea that you can just nip down to Surrey to film unicorns."

"Now you're just being daft. Obviously you don't get unicorns in Surrey." Daniel adjusted the zoom a tiny fraction. He wanted the shot to be perfect. And also for the young woman to have a moment to feel smug too, because he wasn't always a particularly nice man. "You don't get them outside of Wales in the UK these days, what with all the griffons."

"Griffons," Jenna repeated it flatly.

"That's right. As bad as grey squirrels, they are. Driving out the native species. The Scottish Kelpie is nearly extinct too, thanks to them. Some idiot was talking about introducing hippogriffs to prey on them, but that's only going to make things worse."

Jenna shook her head. "How can you say all this like it's… nothing?"

Daniel sighed. Seriously, had he ever been like this? He couldn't remember it if he had. Like most of the rest of the lads back at base camp, he'd more or less popped into being middle-aged. He tried to be kind about it.

"It's not that it's nothing, but it is normal. Me, I've filmed kraken out in the Pacific. I've filmed dragons mating in the Sahara. I worked on that Attenborough one about how tentacled things have taken after foxes and gone urban—not really his best stuff. Eventually, you work out that it's not actually any better than getting shots of lions or rare butterflies. And after that, you realize that whatever you're filming is still just your job—a job that is often, quite frankly, bloody boring."

Jenna shook her head, of course. Daniel had known she would.

"That's just not-"

Glimpsing something through the viewfinder, Daniel put up a hand. "Shut up. I think it's coming."

It came. It was a speck at first—a darker spot against the sun's reflection. Then a brighter spot against the clouds. For all Daniel had said about it, the phoenix didn't fly like a chicken. It didn't even plunge like a dropping hawk. Instead it fell like a meteorite—bright and fast and stunning. A few feet from the earth, it spread its wings and drifted the way a swan might have come in to land, if a swan had been red and wreathed in brilliance. It landed like it knew it had an audience.

Daniel kept the camera on it as it walked a few steps around the nesting site, picking up a few last bits of twigs. The phoenix stacked them on the others around the egg, giving the whole arrangement a look that seemed to be assessing the suitability of the whole arrangement. This was it. Daniel knew it. Deep down in his bones, he knew it.

The bird hopped up onto the nest. It turned right around in a circle, like a cat trying to get comfortable, then finally, it settled, facing Daniel's camera. It couldn't be better. Just another minute or two... just another…

The phoenix spread its wings, and light flared red, then golden, then the blue white of a welding torch. Heat blossomed with it; enough that Daniel could feel it back where he was—enough that he wondered briefly if there would be anything left of the nest camera after this, and how the accounts department would react to that. He didn't wonder it long, though, because at that moment the phoenix sang.

There was no other word for it. The cry of the phoenix as it burned was sweet, and melodic, and it cut right through Daniel as he listened. It sounded exactly like a bird's song should when it had only one moment to convey just how much it was giving up for its young, and just how happy it was about doing that. It was joy, and sadness, and hope—always hope.

And then it was gone. Daniel kept the camera on the nest automatically. Almost as automatically, he clamped one hand around Jenna's arm, pinning her to the earth. The only sounds were the faint crack of eggshell, and the last cracklings of the burnt-out nest.

It emerged unsteadily, trying to work out how you did this "putting one foot in front of the other" business and not quite getting it right. It wasn't as large as its parent, not yet. Its plumage wasn't quite as bright, but it would be. Someday, out around the Sun, it would be. The young phoenix shook out its feathers with the air of someone trying them out. It spread its wings, catching the Sun for a moment, then it looked up at the sphere quizzically.

Finally, with a rapid fluttering, it took to the air. The takeoff wasn't as beautiful as the landing, but there was something perfect about that too. Something perfect about the fact that even phoenix chicks had to take off a little uncertainly—about knowing that eventually this tiny thing, flapping unsteadily above the nest site, would drop like a meteorite too. It circled once, just once, before heading for the Sun. Daniel watched it, filmed it, until it was just a speck again, before he stood up.

Jenna stood up beside him, tears running down her face, her hands balled into fists.

"Don't you dare try to tell me that's nothing," she warned. "Don't you dare!"

Daniel turned away with a shrug. Quietly, making sure that Jenna couldn't see him, he wiped away the tear that had made it halfway down his cheek.

Viva La...

Y'tak sighed as he moved a long finger down his to-do list for the day, and he reflected (not for the first time) on the fact that he was always getting volunteered for things. There had been the job of classroom ant-milk monitor when he had been just a youngling, which was no joke when the ants in question where the size of small hover-vehicles. Then, he had been volunteered for the job of official history collector for the local collective, which was never fun, given how often the official history changed these days. And now…

"Let's see," Y'tak muttered. "Rioting in the streets, check. Contacting the TV stations so that the revolution will be properly televised, check. Headquarters for the revolutionary council, check. List of people to be put against the wall and shot…"

Y'tak looked through his collection of notes, then swore. He was sure that he'd had it there somewhere. He picked up his communication device and rang through to his assistant.

"May'dit, have you got the voting results for the against-the-wall list over there yet?"

"Sure, boss. Do you want me to read it out to you?"

"Send it over. Just give me the highlights for now."

The list included four minor celebrities, a couple of politicians no one had heard of, and of course, the last organizer. Y'tak sighed again as he put the communications unit down. Organizing a revolution really wasn't easy, yet it had to be done, apparently. The same as it did every two years.

Of course, given the job he'd had before, Y'tak knew the history. Two hundred years before, the planet had been suffering under a particularly unpleasant dictatorship, but it had almost risen up to overthrow him, or at least get its hands on the assets in his various bank accounts. There it might have ended, had the totally elected government that followed not turned out to be almost as bad. It lasted less than a year before a second revolution, fueled by anger at the failure of the first, swept it away completely.

The next government lasted approximately six weeks, before finally being brought down in circumstances that weren't entirely clear, but which might have had something to do with the escalation of an argument in a local coffee shop. After that… well, in those first few years, the longest a government had lasted was eighteen months, by the simple expedient of hiding in a fortified bunker and refusing to let anyone in the moment it got into power. It might have gone on a little longer had the air conditioning not broken.

The current system was a lot better than that of course. Y'tak had no doubts about that. Two whole years had passed for each government before the inevitable revolution that had become such a part of political life on the planet—revolutions that had become rather stylized after the fiftieth or so. Now, instead of every member of the outgoing government being slaughtered, along with everyone they had ever met (which had led, among other things, to a drastic shortage of political reporters in the early years), just a token selection of individuals voted for by the public were shot. Those mostly turned out to be reality TV stars.

It was just that there was such a lot to do to organize it. Well, no, it wasn't *just* that. It was the violence and the chaos and the inevitability of being overthrown in due course too. It was the way the limited long-term prospects of the average government made it likely to put in stupid laws just for the sake of it. Just in his lifetime, Y'tak could remember ones that had banned wearing hats on a Wednesday, declared milkshakes the drink of the politically suspect, and insisted that all business meetings should be conducted on the beach.

Then there were the traditions. The wall was one of them, but there were others. The re-writing of the official history, for example. It had probably started off as a serious endeavor to try to persuade people of the new rulers' views, but now it seemed like people were just putting in whatever silliness they thought they could get away with. And they weren't putting in proper references anymore. Oh, and there was the calendar too. Apparently, it had now become traditional for every revolutionary government to change the calendar as much as possible, which was really good news for no one except underwear models. With those constant changes, it was hard to keep track of anything.

Weirdly though, the worst thing was how *little* anything changed. No government stayed in power long enough to effect real change, and any major legislation they did bring in was quickly shot down by the next lot, probably along with a couple of Z-listers and a cheating sports star or two. The end result was a society where nothing of much importance seemed to have altered in at least the last century, even as everything on the surface changed completely every couple of years.

Y'tak's communications unit went off, interrupting his train of thought (oh, and the trains still didn't run on time, no matter what anyone said). He half expected it to be May'dit again, but it turned out to be someone else entirely.

"Hello," the figure on the other end said, "my name is T'idy. Possibly you have heard of me?"

Well, yes. For one thing, Y'tak's assistant had mentioned him just a few minutes ago.

"You organized the last revolution."

"Yes," the other man said, "I had that honor. I just thought I'd check in with you and see if you needed any help with anything. I know what a lonely job it can be, trying to overthrow the established system and bring in a radical new dawn of… well, whatever it is you're bringing in. Does your lot have a manifesto? Mine didn't."

"I think they're too busy trying to work out what to rename February," Y'tak said. "Um, am I really supposed to be talking to you? Only-"

"Almost certainly not," T'idy replied. "On the other hand, what are they going to do? Shoot me? I think you already have that one covered, and there's not really much they can do to you either that won't happen in due course."

Y'tak wasn't sure that he wanted to think about that one. "Look, I'm sorry to be blunt," he said, "but is there anything you want? I have so much to get through, and there isn't much time to do it in. I've still have to organize an inciting event, and you know as well as anyone what it can be like trying to come up with something big enough to justify all this."

"Actually, I went for a more back-to-basics approach for mine," T'idy said. "I just had the revolution and then let the historians argue over what the incitement had been afterwards. You'd be amazed at some of the things they came up with as suggestions too."

Y'tak thought about that for a bit. "You know, that might actually work."

"Of course it will," the other man said over the communications unit. "It's what the last thirty of us have done, after all. At least, that's what my predecessor told me."

"You and the organizer before you talked?" Y'tak asked. It seemed almost shocking, even though he was doing exactly the same.

"Well, yes, of course. It's become something of a tradition, in fact. The… ahem, *outgoing* incumbent always contacts his or her successor, as it were. Just to let them know that there aren't any hard feelings, and so forth."

"But I'm about to have you shot," Y'tak pointed out.

"Oh, that isn't your fault," T'idy said. "Or, at least, it isn't personal—any more than it was personal when I had to have the second runner up of *The Collective Has No Talent* put against the wall. I actually quite enjoyed her music. It's simply the way things go. I'm here to remind you that you are part of a long tradition that is, despite everything, functioning quite well."

"How can you say that it's functioning well," Y'tak argued, "when it's about to get you killed? When we've been killing people for hundreds of years?"

"Perhaps because it *has* been all those years," T'idy suggested. "We have a political system that is fundamentally stable. We wouldn't want to go upsetting that, would we? Anyway, if you find that there is anything you need, please don't hesitate to get in touch. Oh, and if you'd like me to be hiding in a cupboard or anything when the soldiers come round to seize me, please do just say the word."

"Um… no," Y'tak said, "that's fine."

He put the communications unit down and stared straight ahead for a while. T'idy had sounded so… so *resigned* to it all—like all this was simply the way things went. That it *was* just the way things went didn't make it any better, particularly not since, two years from then, it would be the way things would be going for Y'tak.

It occurred to him then why he had probably been chosen for the job. He was exactly the sort of person who could quietly organize things without complaining—who was so used to being put upon that people probably thought it wouldn't make any difference to him being shot afterwards. He wasn't someone to make a fuss. In short, he was exactly the sort of person who could probably be trusted to have the chat T'idy had just had with him with whoever followed him.

Well, what else could he really do? They'd been having revolutions for years now, as regular as clockwork—possibly more so, given the various changes to the calendars. People were *used* to revolutions. One man, even one man determinedly worried about being shot, probably couldn't do very much about it. It was simply the system, and there wasn't much point in trying to go against it.

Y'tak replayed that thought to himself and shook his head ruefully. It didn't change anything though. When it came down to it, what *could* he do? Overthrow the government? That would just mean that he got paid for a job well done. So what else was there?

The appointed morning of the revolution came around with everything as planned. The revolutionary cells were in place; the sympathetic reporters had received their press releases; and the police, army, and librarians were all poised to defect as soon as they got the official authorization to do so. All that was needed now was Y'tak's signal.

He'd been quite clear on that. The operation was such a complex one that a single mistimed element could spell an absolute farce. No one, from the new provisional government to anyone involved in the carefully coordinated displays of precision rioting, was going to move without his say so—which was why he spent the day in a bar with his communications unit set to mute. Oh, he checked it a couple of times. He even sent a few messages back saying that everything was under control and that they should continue to wait, just to be sure. Mostly though, he enjoyed a few quiet drinks, played a couple of games of pool, and even got chatting to a rather cute young woman behind the bar. It was, Y'tak felt, possibly the most revolutionary thing he had done all week.

The revolutionary forces waited for several hours before sloping home in embarrassment. The leaders tried to get the revolution off the ground, but found that they didn't actually want to organize it, given what generally happened to those who did. The press complained, of course, but there didn't seem to be anything anyone could do with it, especially since Y'tak had last been seen heading for a spaceport with a young woman. The crisis continued for almost a week before the previous organizer put forward the slightly old-fashioned idea of holding elections instead. It took a bit of getting used to, but eventually people were prepared to put up with it, especially once a few revisions to the formats of reality shows meant that they could still watch their favorite nobodies being shot.

Tall Tales

So you want to know about Ned, do you? You know, the best thing about working in pubs is always the patrons. You meet some right characters in this game, although they generally aren't the ones who like to *think* of themselves as "characters". Those are what we in the pub management and general landlord-ing trade call "annoying drunks who are lucky they don't get thrown out more often". Mostly, they leave when you put the price of beer up.

The real characters are the ones who never seem to realize what they're like. I've seen them all, I have. The ones who go in for a swift half and miss the whole night. The ones who do Elvis impressions for no good reason, or who carry around a live budgie with them everywhere for no better reason than because the thing doesn't like to be left alone.

And then there's Old Ned.

Ned kind of came with this little place, pretty much the way the bar, or the curtains, or the clapped-out pool table did. He was a respectable looking older guy, maybe sixty, who would always come in the same time every day, wearing a suit and sitting on the same seat at the bar.

Turned out, Ned was one of those guys who liked to tell stories. No, that's not putting it right. He didn't like doing it. He wouldn't do it at all, sober. Sober, he was just a guy who sat by himself and didn't say much. He had a kind of haunted look to him, maybe, but he wasn't any trouble—except maybe a couple of times, but that's later.

Drunk was a different matter. Get Ned drunk, and he'd start to tell anyone who'd listen all kinds of things. The first time I heard him, I assumed he had to be doing something else as well, it was that out there. He told this rambling story about this woman he'd rescued from some flying newt, and how she'd run off with another guy. It took me a good ten minutes to realize that he was talking about rescuing somebody from a dragon, and maybe five after that to stop laughing.

I guess he got that a lot. People would buy him drinks, just to get him drunk enough to start talking. It was just the way he was so serious about it. A normal guy would have cracked a smile or at least given some little nod to say how he knew it was garbage, and he knew you knew it too, but let's all pretend.

But, not Ned. He'd tell some story about kidnapping the queen of the elves the way I'd talk about working the bar of some dive down in the city. He told us about a siege or another with orcs climbing over the battlements and dragons breathing fire down at the defenders. He sounded just like some of the vets we'd get in sometimes—the ones who wanted to drink deep enough that they could forget they ever went anywhere.

Maybe he was a vet too, even though most of us just figured he was some washed up writer with too many stories going around in his head. I saw him once with his sleeves rolled up to play pool, and he had so many marks down his arms—burn marks, knife scars, even what looked like claw marks in one spot… plus a few tattoos, though they were mostly abstract kinds of things, like symbols—not great work, honestly.

I mentioned before that there wasn't much trouble with Ned. Well, there were a couple of times. One of them, young Billy Treveson decided he didn't want to have to get an old man drunk to hear stories. Billy was a big boy, and he grabbed Ned really good and hauled him up onto his feet. The next thing I knew, Billy was out cold before I even had a chance to reach under the bar for the shotgun. People were a bit more polite to Old Ned after that.

The other was a bit stranger. I'd been working that place a while by then. I was just locking up, and Ned came running over, looking like he had half of Hell after him, if you know what I mean. He begged me to let him inside before "they" find him. I asked him what he was talking about, hinting that if he was going to go and get drunk somewhere else, he should go sleep it off before he came back to my place. He just looked round wildly. It was then that I saw something, or I think I saw something, or I don't quite see something. I'm not sure which. I only know that suddenly I was sure there was something out there—or someone, maybe.

I asked him at the time if it was some kind of gang thing. I'm not sure why. I mean, Ned, in a gang? But there were all those funny tattoos of his, and well… what else was I going to think? Anyway, he shook his head, so I let him inside. Frankly, I kind of wanted to be inside right then, too. So we went in, and sat at the bar. After a while, I couldn't help myself, so I started serving him drinks. I didn't get much out of him though—just some stupid story about being chased by the shadows of ten evil men he'd killed way back.

Still, it wore away the time. After a bit, he said it was as safe as it was ever going to be, so I went home. So did he, I guess; although for some reason, I couldn't help remembering the bit on the news the next day about some old factory exploding. You might have seen it. No, well, you obviously aren't from around here, so you probably wouldn't.

Are you on the way to some kind of convention? The great battle. Oh, like one of those renaissance faire things? No? Where are you from, anyway? No, don't answer that. Just tell me what you want with Ned. I mean, he might be a bit weird, but he's basically a nice guy, you know. I wouldn't want to go around causing trouble for him. You want him to help overthrow the powers of darkness? Yeah, seriously, buddy, what do you want him for?

Listen, a jokes a joke, but I've had enough. I'm not a violent guy, but... oh. Oh, right. Um... nice sword—especially the way it's on fire like that. And the girl with the pointy ears holding lightning in between her hands like that? Very... impressive. So Ned is... Edward of the Sundered Tower, you say? Magus of the Battle of Skarn, Defender of the Broken Pass, troll slayer, and a couple of other titles you can't quite remember? That's... um, impressive. He *really-*

I'll just go and fetch him, shall I? I think he's in the back somewhere.

Villainy

"Now then, Max," Uncle Andy said, "let's get you settled in. I know things can be a bit worrisome on your first day, but you'll soon find yourself feeling comfortable."

Max Zade nodded. Nervous didn't begin to cover it. After all, a young man starting out in almost any field would have been nervous. One starting out in the field of super villainy, on the other hand, presumably had a right to feel distinctly uncomfortable about the whole thing—not least of all because of the tight black costume and mask that had clearly been designed with awe-inspiring terror in mind rather than fitting well. Still, you didn't complain on your first day—particularly not when the man you would be complaining to was Andreas Marrus, better known as the Shadowed Cape—a man who had once stolen most of Newark for a bet and who had held his own against some of the top heroes in the business, according to the stories he and Max's father had always told. This was not a man who would be phased by the mere requirements of villainous costuming.

"If the mask is itching too much, you can always take it off," Uncle Andy said. "It's not like there's anyone else here, and those things always itch something awful until they settle in. Why do you think I went with this?"

He spun, showing off the deep, inky darkness of the long cloak he wore, complete with hood.

"Um, I thought that was all about inspiring awe," Max said.

"Nah. Mostly, it's because I can put the hood up. No need for a mask, see. Course, if I'd had any sense, I would have been the Shadowed Anorak, but it's a bit late to change at my time of life. Now, hurry up. I'm meant to give you the tour before I introduce you to the lads."

"The tour" was an actual tour of the Secret Isle—that most carefully hidden base that served as a home to almost every super villain in the area at some point, usually while they were between giant robot-infested underground complexes. It was rumored to be so secret that even after fifty years, no hero had ever worked out where it was. It was the dark heart of almost all genuinely super villainy for miles around. There were people, mostly people who worked in comic book stores, admittedly, who would have killed for the chance to have a look around.

It was just a pity Max wasn't one of them, really.

It had always been assumed that he would be going into villainy, because when your father was Zackary Zane, the Mad Professor himself, there were some things that just seemed obvious. Max had known his future career in the same way that he had known that gravity would stay on (except around a couple of his father's more ingeniously diabolical devices) and that the sun would shine (ditto). He had grown up adjusting giant evil robot parts on his father's black clad knee. His first car had had spikes on the wheels. The idea that he might want to grow up to be, for example, an accountant had simply never been entertained at home—not even in the big pit with the piranha in it, reserved for heroes and people who came round trying to sell encyclopedias.

The trouble was, he occasionally suspected that it might have been nice if he had been given that choice—not about the accountancy, because there were some things too unpleasant even for him to contemplate, but a choice, nonetheless. It wasn't as if he even liked the idea of evil. His father might have brought him up with stories of mutant lobsters and secret bases, but his mother had brought Max up with a strong sense of right and wrong to go with it. Max wasn't sure how the two fit together.

Yet, here he was, following the Shadowed Cape around the Secret Isle, looking at a bunch of other things that deserved their capital letters, from Ultimate Secret Labs (time to be booked in advance) to the Scanner of Doom (to be manned according to the rota—double shifts on Tuesdays).

"And this is the canteen," Uncle Andy said. "Don't eat anything Chef Death offers you, and if something in the fridge looks like Jell-O, test that it isn't a mutant acid monster before you take a spoon to it. Now, there's somewhere you really should see."

He led Max to a room where everything was covered in old sheets, peeling one off to reveal an array of what looked like junk to Max—quite familiar looking junk, but junk, nonetheless.

"What is all this?" Max asked.

Uncle Andy flicked a switch, and the junk moved, forming itself into a vaguely avian shape. "Your father's workshop. Don't you remember his robot chicken minions?"

Max did. His dad had brought one home once. It had squawked its way around the living room before punching a chicken shaped hole in the wall. It had been one of his dad's crazier schemes. He pulled one or two other sheets away, revealing other things belonging to the past. There was the anti-gravity ray he'd won his first science fair with. There was the suit of power armor Dad had let him play basketball in once. So many memories... Maybe too many.

Uncle Andy seemed to sense it. "Come on," he said. "It's time we went to meet the rest of the boys."

The boys turned out to be quite a collection, though a collection of what, Max wasn't entirely sure, as Uncle Andy took him through to a small games room to introduce them. There were a number of older gentlemen Max vaguely recognized from barbeques and visits, although on those occasions, they hadn't been wearing nearly so much in the way of masks and badly ironed spandex—which was probably just as well really. Max knew their names. There was the Destructor, the Twins of Doom, and the Spinning Vortex, who sat on a swivel chair, turning happily round and round.

"Poor chap hasn't really been the same since his fight with the mighty Clang," Uncle Andy explained. "Just sits there. Still, someone has to look after the old boy. There's not much of a pension in villain-ing, Max. Come on… there's still the younger crowd to meet."

The younger crowd turned out to be mostly around Max's age or a little older. They were exclusively male. Most of them had acne scars, and a couple were so overweight that the only way Max could imagine them terrorizing a city was by sitting on it.

"That's Fat Man and *The* Fat Man," Uncle Andy said. "Don't get them confused. They're busy arguing over who gets the name. Apparently, the loser has to go on a diet."

Of the rest, there was one fairly spindly young man, who wore an elaborate costume, but he seemed to be doing so mostly to disguise the fact that he didn't have any muscles under it; one who looked around nervously every few seconds, jumping whenever there was a sound; and a couple who seemed to be wearing costumes that seemed fairly familiar. It took Max a moment to realize that it was because they were wearing almost exactly the same black and silver armor arrangement that his father had favored.

"Your old man is still a big name with the young ones," Uncle Andy explained. "Although it might be nice if one of them picked out a decent cape now and again. You didn't fancy the armor?"

Max shook his head. "I… not really. So they got into this just because of my dad?"

"Oh, not *just* because of him, I'd guess. They probably thought it would help get them girls too."

Max looked around pointedly at the space that currently contained precisely no examples of the female of the species. Uncle Andy caught the look and grinned.

"I said that they 'thought it', not that it was true—not these days, anyway." He sighed. "The villainy business isn't what it once was, boy. Time was, a man could raise a small army of minions, take over half a country, and generally cause mayhem just by snapping his fingers. These days, you're hard pushed to be more than a nuisance, unless you're one of the groups that gets government grants."

Max's eyebrows made a dash for his hairline. "We're government subsidized?"

"Of course we are, boy. How else do you think we afford this kind of place? Some people at least understand that you've got to have villains—not like some of the heroes you get nowadays."

Max wasn't sure he understood. Why would the government pay villains? Why would people idolize villains like Max's father, to the extent of dressing up like them? After all, what they did was *wrong,* wasn't it? Max had an excuse, in the fact that his dad had pushed him into it as surely as a killer robot could push down bank walls, but even that felt paper thin, sometimes. So why were the rest of them bothering with it?

He took a breath. "Uncle Andy, there's something I have to ask you."

"Just down the end there… on the left."

"What?"

"The lavatories. Only be quick, because we've got a shout to go on in a minute. You're paired with me for the day. I thought you'd want someone to show you the ropes."

"That…" Max considered telling the older man that wasn't what he had been asking, thought better of it, and nodded. "That would be great."

They went out in Uncle Andy's old minivan, which wasn't the most villainous form of transportation, until you considered the thought that what a real villain needed was plenty of room for whatever hideous creations he had come up with this week. Together, they headed for the city's central plaza, found a parking space, and got out.

"Now," Uncle Andy said, "what we're meant to be doing is terrorizing a few innocent civilians. I've brought a fairly standard death ray with me, but you're going to have to improvise."

"A death ray?" Max asked. He was perfectly comfortable with two of those three words. The middle one, however, was giving him some trouble. He wasn't sure if he wanted to go around killing people.

"Oh, don't worry; it's just for show. We'd lose our funding if we went around just killing people any old how. It's bad for business. Now all we have to do is pick out a likely spot." Uncle Andy pointed to a group of Japanese tourists, all happily snapping away at statues on the outside of the city gallery with the enthusiasm of people who clearly believed that vacations only counted if you had proof afterwards. "They look like a good place to begin."

Max still wasn't sure that he understood. But from the sounds of it, the Shadowed Cape didn't plan on disintegrating anyone in the immediate future, so Max decided to go along with things, at least for now. He took a determined step forward.

"Actually, wait a second," Uncle Andy said. "I've just got to nip inside."

Beneath his mask, Max's brow furrowed. "Why?"

"Do I need to draw you a map, kid? Honestly, it used to be that my biggest enemy was Captain Marvelousness, not my damn prostate. Don't start anything while I'm gone. This is meant to be a two-man gig."

Uncle Andy hurried off. There was a small café next to the gallery, with seats outside, so Max sat down, ordered a coffee, and started to wait. He'd been waiting for about a minute when he decided that, as he wasn't technically doing anything villainous, there wasn't much point in wearing his mask—especially since it was itching. He took it off and put it down on the table, just as a shadow fell over it.

"You shouldn't really do that," a voice said. "You never know who might be watching."

Max looked up. The figure standing before his table was a woman—quite definitely so. There was absolutely no way that Max could have been mistaken on that score, given her costume. It was blue. There wasn't very much of it.

"Are you quite done staring?"

"Sorry," Max said. The woman was dark haired and beautiful, even with a mask covering her eyes. Frankly, it was about the only bit of her that was covered. She appeared to be a year or two older than Max, but not much more than that.

"Villains don't say sorry," the woman said. She looked Max over. "Are you new?"

"Yes," Max admitted. "Does it show?"

“Maybe a bit. I’m Veronica of the Silver Flame.” She extended a hand. Max took it.

“Max Zane.”

Veronica smiled just a little. “I bet everyone makes a comment about your father at this point.”

“Pretty much.”

“And it explains what you’re doing on the villains’ side of things rather than going over to be a hero. You look the heroic type, you know.”

Max considered the traditionally square jawed, hypertrophic archetype. “Um… thanks, I guess. Sorry, I have to ask. Are we supposed to be fighting?”

Veronica shrugged. Max tried not to stare. “We can if you like, but my partner isn’t here just yet. I saw yours go into the gallery, so unless you’re playing the lookout for a cunning heist, I’d rather just get a coffee, if that’s okay.”

“Sure.”

Veronica sat down and ordered an espresso. The waiter who brought it clearly didn’t know where to look.

“So, have you been a super-hero long?” Max asked.

Veronica smiled. “That sounds a lot like ‘do you come here often?’ But no, I haven’t. A year, maybe. Before that, I actually tried being a villain.”

Max tried to think of the polite thing to say. “It wasn’t for you?”

“Not really. I mean, I got to the point where I was asking myself what it was all for.”

Max nodded. "I know what you mean."

"*You* know what I mean? The son of Zackary Zane?" Veronica looked at him for a second or two. "Then again, I guess you would. People just assumed, didn't they?"

Max nodded. "The worst part is that I'm not sure what the point of it all is. I mean, what are villains actually *for*?"

"Well, it's not too late to become a hero," Veronica said. "Seriously, you should think about it. You'd probably be good at it. You, at least, don't have the obvious problem I did with the villainy."

"What's that?" Max asked.

"The costumes. Honestly, it's like people can't see a villainess without assuming that she's going to want to dress like some kind of cut-price dominatrix. It was embarrassing."

Max tried not to imagine Veronica dressed like that. He failed. "I can't help noticing that your um… current costume is a bit…"

"The villains' ones were worse," Veronica said firmly, then looked over at the other side of the square. "Here comes my boss."

A figure strode over. He was made for striding—also for posing, probably on the covers of things. His costume was the same bright blue as Veronica's, and it had so many muscles rippling beneath that it looked like a sack stuffed with coconuts. He paused several times to sign autographs.

When he got to the table, he looked at Max with obvious disdain, flicking a proprietary glance over at Veronica.

"What are you doing here, evildoer?" he demanded. "Do you not know that Commander Perfection is here to protect the city?"

"Um…" Max stood up, unsure of exactly how he was meant to respond to that. Too late, he remembered his mask and scrambled to put it on.

"And what were you doing with my protégé?" Commander Perfection demanded. "Trying to seduce her back to the ways of evil?"

At 'seduce' Max found himself blushing. Thankfully, he'd gotten his mask back in place by then.

"No… I… we were just talking."

"Aha!"

There were people that actually *said* 'aha'?

"I know your game, evildoer."

"Look, would you stop calling me that?" Max asked.

"Trying to distract my beautiful, but essentially easily deceived assistant, from her duties, while your compatriot sneaks into the gallery?"

"He just went in to use the-"

"What do they call you, evildoer? I will need to know for when I hand you over to the police."

"It's Max," Max said. "Max Zane. Look, are you really planning to hand me over to the police? I haven't actually done anything-"

But it seemed that Veronica's friend wasn't listening. He swung a punch at Max, and his fist travelled with the kind of blurring speed that you have when you spent more time hitting the weight room than you probably should. At the sight of it steaming towards his now masked face, Max momentarily froze in panic. Then he reacted.

Specifically, he reacted in the way his father had taught him to react over long and occasionally painful hours during his childhood. He swayed out of the way of the incoming punch, caught the wrist, executed a precise twist, and sent Commander Perfection flying into the table Max had just been drinking at. When the man got up, Max ducked his sudden rush, straightening up at just the right moment to send the super-hero sprawling once more, leaving him groaning on the floor.

He looked around and saw Veronica standing there open mouthed.

"What… what are you doing? That… that's not allowed."

Max wasn't sure he understood. "I'm just-"

A hand clamped down onto his shoulder. Max was halfway into a complicated wrist lock before he realized that it was the Shadowed Cape, and not his heroic opponent. It was hard to judge Uncle Andy's expression with his hood up, but somehow, Max got the impression that he wasn't happy. Max couldn't see why.

"I've got this," Uncle Andy said—not to him but to the idiot currently sprawled out on the ground. "I'm sorry. He doesn't know what he's meant to be doing just yet. I'll deal with this. I'm sorry."

Max wasn't sorry, but as Uncle Andy led him away from the scene of the fight, his hand still clamped firmly on Max's shoulder, he got the feeling that he was going to be.

"What did you think you were *playing* at?" Uncle Andy demanded, once they were both back at the Secret Isle.

"What?" Max demanded. "He tried to punch me, *and* he's a hero. I thought we were meant to fight heroes?"

"We're not meant to *win!"* the older man shouted back. "Except occasionally, as a heightening the tension plot device, against minor characters. Honestly, did your father teach you nothing?"

Max shrugged. "Actually, he was the one who taught me that move. Look, I don't see-"

"No, you don't, do you?" Uncle Andy stared at him. "And I bet Zackary never taught you about the code, either. He hated the code when they introduced it. He didn't see that it's the only way we can live these days—the only thing we're good for."

"What code?" Max demanded. "What are you talking about?"

"I knew it," Uncle Andy sighed, and he gestured to a couple of the chairs in the island's recreation room. Max sat down. "I *knew* he hadn't told you. Honestly, Zackary will be the death of me one of these days. Although actually, with that resurrection machine of his, I suppose that technically-"

"What code?" Max prompted the older man, not wanting to be there all day.

"It's fairly simple really," Uncle Andy said. "What do you think villains are for, when it gets down to it?"

"Um…" Max had been thinking about that one a lot. He still didn't have an answer.

"Mostly, so that there can be heroes." Uncle Andy looked out at nothing in particular. "We didn't understand that in the old days. We just got on with things. But what we didn't realize was that we were just a part of the whole story—a story the good guys have to win, if they're going to serve as an example to people."

"So the code…"

"I'm getting to it. For a few years, things got a bit quiet. Modern policing meant that villains could generally be caught without the need for someone prancing about in tights. The trouble was, while that might have reduced the number of villains about, it also reduced the ability of heroes to inspire people. Things got bad for a while, or so they tell me. I was busy working the kinks out of an idea for a secret base inside the shell of an oversized turtle."

It made a kind of sense to Max. Well, the bit without the turtle did, anyway. "So what changed?" he asked Uncle Andy.

"Oh, some clever type in government saw the importance of heroes, and they saw the importance of villains *to* heroes. With the result, they came up with the code: We do villainy, but only on a strictly organized basis and only on the proviso that we agree to lose to the heroes in the end."

"So when I beat Commander Perfect back there," Max said, "that was against the code?"

"About as far against it as you can get," the older man confirmed, rearranging his cape. "Frankly, I don't think it will be a problem. We'll probably just get a slap on the wrists for it, but technically, things could be bad."

Max wondered what the Shadowed Cape might consider bad. Then he found out, because an explosion shook the room they sat in. Max grabbed Uncle Andy, dragging him out of the way as large chunks of wall went flying beside them.

"Bad like that, you mean?"

Alarms began to sound, presumably not so much because there was any possibility that anyone on the Secret Isle wouldn't have noticed what was happening, but more so because there are some situations where you have to have alarms. Oh, and smoke. You had to have smoke too, apparently, in quantities that made it hard for Max to see where he was going.

Through the smoke strode figures. Max recognized some of them. There was the bright pink form of The Big, which came out every time some scientist or another felt embarrassed. There was Butterfly Man, and The Accountant, and there, towards the back, were Veronica and Commander Perfection, who was throwing around either Fat Man or The Fat Man, Max couldn't remember which, as though he didn't weigh much at all.

As the smoke started to clear, Max could see that there was fighting everywhere. The Accountant was doing something unpleasant with a double entry ledger to one of the Twins of Doom, while Butterfly Man fought the other. A blurring figure was darting around the Spinning Vortex, making him whirl faster and faster. Commander Perfection was throwing around the Secret Isle's other oversized inhabitant, now, and Destructor was sprawled against one of the nearest walls, having apparently run straight at Veronica.

Max moved over to her, and he just about managed to parry a kick aimed at his head.

"What are you doing?" he demanded.

"What I have to do," she shot back. "I'm not the one who went and messed things up for everyone."

She went at him with a volley of punches, which Max had to roll backwards to avoid. He grabbed another kick, spun Veronica, and pulled her into a hold for a moment.

"Look, I know I broke the rules, and I'm sorry, but I didn't even *know.*"

"*I* know that," Veronica said, "but do you think that matters to him?" She nodded towards Commander Perfection. "You made him look stupid, and now he's invoking the whole code stuff. Look, I'm sorry about this, but I have to go along with it, or they'll think I'm going back over to villainy. I am *not* putting up with those costumes again."

She did something that sent Max sprawling over her shoulder, and as he sprang back to his feet, he realized that things were quiet. But then, he supposed, what did he expect? After all, most of the villains there had had long practice in losing, and they were currently crumpled up, having been soundly beaten. Besides him, only one other black clad figure was still standing.

Max walked over to where Uncle Andy stood, in front of Commander Perfection. Because Uncle Andy currently had his hood up, it was impossible for Max to read his expression.

"You didn't need to do this," the older man said to the hero.

Commander Perfection shrugged. “I think we did. I think you villains needed to be reminded of where you stand in all of this, or did you think that there wouldn’t be any comeback for what you did out in the square?”

“That was all me,” Max said, pushing forward. “I did it. I didn’t know about the code. I’m sorry.”

“You expect me to believe that?” Commander Perfection scowled as he said it.

“It’s true, Barry,” Veronica said. “I was talking to him before it happened, remember.”

“I told you not to call me that. And why are you standing up for him, anyway? Not going back over to the dark side, are you?”

“You know I’m not, *Commander.* It’s just… we’re heroes. We should be about telling the truth, right?”

“We should be about pounding evil into the dirt,” Commander Perfection shot back.

Max tried hard not to think of him as Barry now that Veronica had let the name slip. It wasn’t easy.

Barry, er, Commander Perfection continued, “I’ll tell you what, though. If the kid didn’t know the code before, maybe he does now?”

“He does,” Uncle Andy assured him. “I saw to it myself.”

Max sighed. “So what? You want to beat me up, is that it? You want to make up for my kicking your ass before?”

Commander Perfection didn’t glare at him. Probably, Max should have taken that as a warning. “No kid. I’ve got a better idea. You can stand there while I give this old fool the beating he deserves. And he isn't going to fight back, because he knows you'll all lose your funding if he does."

The blue clad hero started towards Uncle Andy. Veronica stepped forward.

"Barry-"

"I *said* don't call me that. Now shut up, Veronica. I'm in charge here. And if you can't shut up, you can go and take your lumps with the other villains. I got you out of that, remember?"

For a moment, Veronica looked like she might say something. Then she winced and stepped back out of the way. Max wanted to call her a coward for doing it, but he didn't, because he knew he was in just the same position. He couldn't do anything—not unless he wanted to ruin things for all of them. He couldn't. But he couldn't stand there either, not as Commander Perfection pulled back his arm to hit the Shadowed Cape. So he ran. He ran from the Secret Isle's common room, hardly caring where he was going and trying very hard not to look back.

Max ended up in his father's old workshop. He wasn't sure why he'd run there, except that the old man had always seemed to have all the answers. What answer would he have had for this though? The Mad Professor had hated the code, according to Uncle Andy. He wouldn't understand the need not to interfere. He wouldn't understand how bad that could be for all of them.

Yet without that code, what was he? What were villains for? Without it, weren't they just thugs, taking what they wanted? Max wasn't sure that he could be that. It wasn't just that people would truly hunt them down, the way they had when his father had been alive. It was that he would be on the wrong side. You couldn't know right from wrong and still choose wrong, could you?

Why not, though? His father had. His father had fought more heroes and come up with more plans than almost anyone else, yet he hadn't been an evil man. He had always been a kind father, and he had been a loving husband to Max's mother.

"What is it for, Dad?" Max demanded aloud. Maybe if he said it loud enough, it would drive out the sound of Commander Perfection's fist hitting Uncle Andy. Just the thought of it made his knuckles tighten. He couldn't do this. He *couldn't.* And in that moment, he understood. Though exactly what he could do about it, Max didn't…

He looked around at the sheets and smiled. Why not?

It was another couple of minutes before Max strode back through the doors to the common area. He was striding more than usual, because powered armor did that, but not necessarily quickly, because he was having to be careful not to tread on any robot chickens. Commander Perfection was still there with the other heroes. Most of the villains from the island were there too, still on the floor, having the sense to stay down. Veronica stood near the back wall, with her hand over her mouth.

And Uncle Andy lay on the floor, just a shapeless lump beneath a black cape. While Max stared at that broken form, Commander Perfection looked over at him.

"What's this? What do you think you're going to do, kid? Haven't you been paying attention?"

"I've been paying attention," Max said. "I've also been thinking."

Veronica took a step forward. "Max, you can't do this. The villains don't win. That's not what they're there for."

Max turned to face her. "You're wrong. Do you want to know what villains are *really* there for?"

"Looking good in black corsetry?" Veronica shot back.

Max shook his head, then looked pointedly at where Uncle Andy lay unmoving. "No. It's simpler than that. We're here to stop heroes. We're here to make sure that there's somebody between the world and people like Barry here. Because without us, I dread to think what the world would be like." He looked down at his father's robots, and took a breath. "Get them."

As the small horde of robotic chicken minions leapt forward, engulfing Commander Perfection, he saw Veronica nod, just once.

Quests

Emsley tried not to give off any signs of panic as he sat outside the office of the head of the cartographers' guild, staring at the map on the wall with the inevitable red arrow showing exactly how close he was to being shouted at. That was what being called into the offices meant, after all, when you were a junior cartographer. It meant that you'd put something in the wrong place on one of your maps, or used the symbol for deciduous trees when you should have used pines, or put in 'here be dragons' when there were in fact only wyverns, and you valued your hide too much to get any closer. Though frankly, Emsley would rather have had the dragons than the guild master's office.

The biggest problem was that he couldn't even remember doing anything wrong. If he'd made a mistake, then he could have had an apology or an explanation ready to bring out the moment he got through the door. It wouldn't have worked, given the guild's motto of *absolute accuracy,* but he might at least have been able to judge accurately whether what he had done was the sort of thing that would earn him a slap on the wrists, or the sort that would see him told, by the people who could tell him it definitively, to get lost.

Instead, Emsley just had to sit there, waiting until the door to the guild master's office opened to reveal Mr. Thwaite—second in command of the guild, and a man whose rotund appearance belied his ability to map in at least six dimensions at once.

"There you are, young Emsley. We've been waiting for you. Come in, please."

Friendly, but of course, that just made it worse. Friendliness just meant that Emsley still didn't know how much trouble he was in. It probably meant, in fact, that he was in so much trouble that the leaders of the guild wanted to savor the look on his face when they finally decided to shout at him.

The guild master's office was dominated by a large oak table on which sat a map of the hundred kingdoms. Behind it sat Mr. Thwaite, along with Guildmaster Gurney, who was rumored to be so old that his first maps had been chipped into stone—much like his expression. There was a chair on the other side of the desk. Emsley sat on it.

"Do you know why you are here, Emsley?" the guild master asked.

"Um… is it the thing with my map of the thieves' guild, sir? Only, if they don't *tell* me about the secret passages-"

"It's not about that, Emsley."

"Or the *N* dimensional mapping of-"

"This is not about any of your work, young Emsley," Mr. Thwaite said. "As far as I can tell, your work has been outstanding for one of your age. That is why the guild master and I have a special task for you."

"A special task?" Emsley briefly flushed with pride, before wondering what, in a guild that occasionally involved mapping out exactly where all the deadfalls were in assorted dungeons, could count as special.

"There have been complaints…" the guild master said. When he spoke, his words fell into place with precision and control. "…from heroes."

"Quite enthusiastic complaints in some cases," Mr. Thwaite put in. "We are still getting the bloodstains out of the lower-west dining room."

"Thank you, Mr. Thwaite," Guildmaster Gurney said, before looking at Emsley. "The heroes in question were complaining about some of our maps. Oh, nothing you have worked on. In fact, you are here precisely because this is a matter that requires a fresh pair of eyes."

"Talking of which," Mr. Thwaite added, "while we were cleaning the dining room, we never did find-"

"Thank you, Mr. Thwaite." The guild master steepled his fingers. "It seems, Emsley, that someone has been providing maps to locations of adventure. They have been placing them in all the authorized guild positions: pinned to the walls of inns with knives, placed in the hands of mysterious men about to collapse in front of heroic bands, and so forth. And yet, those maps do *not* in fact lead to any such place. Heroes have been getting to the large spot marked X only to find that there *is* no trap filled dungeon there, no ravening dragon, and so forth. You can imagine how that makes us look. *Absolute accuracy,* Emsley, that is our motto, and someone is making a mockery of it, if these reports are to be believed."

"Someone is making inaccurate maps?" Emsley asked in a hushed tone. Just the idea of it was enough to make him feel a little uncomfortable—although that might have also had something to do with the fact that the chair he was in seemed to have started life as some kind of torture device.

"It has happened before," Mr. Thwaite said. "A decade ago, there was the great advertising crisis. You may have heard of it."

Emsley had. Someone had put out maps promising great treasure for brave heroes, and each one had led unfailingly to 'Honest Joe's House of Stuff'. It had been a dark day indeed.

"This is worse," the guild master said. "Then, there was at least something there, and the proprietor of the shop in question could hardly complain when assorted heroes proceeded to rob him blind. Now, though, there *is* no destination, leaving a bunch of disgruntled heroes on the street. Can you imagine that, Emsley?"

Emsley nodded. He could imagine it all too easily. He had once had the misfortune to be walking past a designated 'heroic' inn around closing time. He had very nearly been hit by a flying elven bard, propelled with some force by a man in furry underwear and too many leather straps.

"So what's happening, sir?"

The guild master pushed a piece of paper across the table between them. "That, Emsley, is what we want you to find out. This is one of the most recent maps to be complained about. Obviously, senior members of the guild cannot be seen to be caught up in such a potential disgrace, so instead, we want *you* to investigate. Go to the spot marked X and report back on what you see. Perhaps there will be clues there as to what is happening. And if you do find it out, maybe we could see about making you a full cartographer, eh?"

Emsley raised an eyebrow at that last bit of encouragement. It took a lot to be promoted from junior cartographer and be let into the innermost secrets of the guild, such as what those stripy poles were actually for. Even without it though, he would have welcomed this mission. If someone was making inaccurate maps, they had to be stopped.

Emsley jumped to his feet, giving the traditional 'left a bit, right a bit' salute of the guild. "At once, Guildmaster. I'll soon find out what is going on!"

Emsley had no idea what was going on. He looked around, then looked down at the map in his hands. He was definitely in the right place. He knew that with the certainty of any member of a guild that went in for orienteering rather than orientation. By rights, looking at the map, he should have been standing at the entrance to a rather large dungeon of doom, full of traps and wandering monsters.

Instead, he was in a field. There were cows. As wandering monsters went, they were a little disappointing, although they at least meant Emsley had to be a little careful where he was putting his feet. They certainly weren't what had been promised by the map.

This all meant that the guild master had been right. Someone was producing inaccurate maps. Not just *inaccurate* maps... there were empty fields all around Emsley, giving him a good view out to the horizon. In all that space, there was no sign of anything remotely dungeon like. There weren't even any signs of building work, suggesting that one was about to be built. This wasn't just a case of the promised dungeon being elsewhere then. The map was an outright fake.

In turn, this meant that someone was cheating the guild and trying to make it look bad deliberately. That wasn't a good thought. Whole adventuring careers had been built on the maps the guild supplied, and with them, the guild's reputation. If people started to believe that those maps couldn't be trusted… well, Emsley didn't want to think about how bad things could be. People wouldn't know where they were. And when you didn't know where you were, how could you ever go anywhere? How could commerce continue, if merchants couldn't move between cities? How could royal processions process, or monstrous hordes ravage properly? No, life would simply grind to a halt.

Emsley had to find out what was going on. He tried to formulate a plan of action. The trouble was that he could see what his plan of action was going to have to be, and it involved rather more action than he'd had in mind. He was going to have to go around to heroic inns, ducking carefully as he went in to avoid the inevitable thrown battle axe, and look for signs that people had been sticking maps to walls before asking the barkeeps for information. And, given what invariably happened when someone asked the barkeeps of such places for information, he was also probably going to have to huddle under a table while the ensuing brawl took place.

Then he'd probably have to track down a few mysterious figures to see if they had been offered any cut price maps by other mysterious figures, go into the heart of some thieves' den or other in search of a cloaked informant who would turn out to be someone's missing brother, and almost certainly end up hanging by his ankles over a big pit full of spikes.

Of course, it *might* not happen like that. It was just about conceivable that Emsley might simply ask questions and get answers, but in his heart of hearts, he knew that things were never that straightforward in the hundred kingdoms. Even if he just put a request for information out with one of the town criers, he would probably end up receiving notes forcing him to meet strangers at midnight under a bridge, where they would inevitably be found dead before someone took Emsley hostage. It was just the way things worked.

It was heroism. Emsley didn't have much time for heroism, on the whole. It was one of the reasons he'd joined the guild. You still got to go out and see the world, the same way you would if you took up the sword, but people in far too much black weren't generally trying to decapitate you when you were standing behind a theodolite. Mostly, they were too busy asking you what it was.

As such, it almost came as a relief to Emsley when someone stepped up behind him and jabbed the point of a crossbow bolt into the small of his back. Almost. Well, no, not almost. Probably, the opposite of almost, really. Actually, not at all, in fact, but at least it saved a lot of messing about.

Emsley raised his hands carefully. "I *knew* this would happen at some point."

Ten minutes later, Emsley found himself sitting on a tree stump near the edge of one of the fields while a cloaked and hooded figure stood in front of him. Emsley wasn't sure whether it planned to kill him or not. It wasn't pointing the crossbow at him, but frankly, that might just mean that it had heard about Emsley's athletic abilities, and knew it had all the time in the world to raise it again.

"Now that we are alone, young Emsley, we can talk."

Emsley knew that voice. He'd been talking to it back at the guild not that long ago, after all. "Mr. Thwaite?"

The hooded figure lowered his hood, revealing the features of the guild's second in command. "Ah, good. It means I don't have to wear this anymore. I always feel like such a fraud, going with the old 'mysterious stranger' routine, given what I'm doing."

"And what are you…" Emsley began, but stopped as Mr. Thwaite produced a rolled-up piece of parchment. It looked identical to the one that had led him there. "You? You're the one producing the fake maps?"

Mr. Thwaite nodded. "Although I prefer to think of them less as fake than as simply fulfilling a vital purpose."

Fulfilling a vital purpose? Mr. Thwaite, who had presumably helped to swear in hundreds of young cartographers, was going against everything the guild stood for as far as Emsley could see. He was making a mockery of the standards of accuracy demanded of true mapmaking, and producing maps that didn't have the dungeons they said they had at their centers.

On the other hand, he was still holding the crossbow.

"Vital purpose." Emsley forced himself to nod. "Right. Obviously."

"I know you don't understand," Mr. Thwaite said. "You are, after all, fully committed to everything the guild stands for."

"And you aren't?" Emsley asked.

"I am committed to the wellbeing of the kingdoms."

"Great," Emsley said. "Um…"

"How do I achieve that with these maps?" Mr. Thwaite guessed. "It is very simple. Tell me, what do you think is the biggest threat to the hundred kingdoms at the moment."

Emsley furrowed his brow with effort. If the man with the crossbow wanted him to think, then he was going to give it a good old-fashioned try.

"Well, there was that thing with the volcano and those short people who wanted to-"

"Not that."

"What about that ancient god who woke up and was going to eat all the kingdoms' vowels? If we hadn't directed it to Wales in time…"

"Not that, either. I'm talking about heroes, Emsley." Mr. Thwaite paused, as though he was waiting for a flash of perfectly timed lightning—or at least for Emsley to understand. Neither happened. "You must have seen what they're like, strutting around towns, throwing fireballs with complete disregard for safety regulations, and generally causing trouble."

Emsley thought back to a few of the heroic bars he'd thought he was going to have to go into. It was true that they were generally a touch on the boisterous side. "But heroes aren't too bad," he insisted.

"Not when they have plenty of quests to keep them occupied, perhaps," Mr. Thwaite said. "Quests give them a purpose. They turn their frankly rather dangerous approach to the subject of social skills into something occasionally useful. At the very least, they tuck them away in dungeons, where they can't really hurt anybody. Figuratively speaking."

"That doesn't explain why you've been making up fake quests," Emsley pointed out. "If anything, the last thing we want to do if you're right is give them *fake* quests, because that will only annoy them. They need the real sort."

"But what if there aren't enough to go around?" Mr. Thwaite looked at him thoughtfully. "Hmm?"

"But for that to happen-"

"It would need the continuous attentions of a great many heroes over a great many years," Mr. Thwaite said. "Unfortunately, it just so happens that the hundred kingdoms has *had* the attentions of a great many heroes over a great many years. Frankly, for the last couple of decades, you've barely been able to move without knocking into a barbarian from the frozen wastes, or an elven song fencer, or such. And generally, they aren't the kind of person you want to knock into."

"Um…"

"The result of all this," Mr. Thwaite went on, "is that, for every legitimate dungeon or pit of doom still filled with monsters, there are a dozen more sitting empty. Heroes had started to sit around with time on their hands. And do you know what happens when heroes have time on their hands, young Emsley?"

"Um… trouble?"

"Exactly. They get restless, and then generally, so do their swords. So I thought, if I could only find a way to harness those tendencies… I know that this goes against guild rules, young Emsley, but I thought that sending them off on heroic journeys with no object was the right thing to do. I'm sure if you think about it, you'll agree."

Emsley thought. He thought about what Mr. Thwaite had said, and how hard it must have been for the man to say it. He thought about the crossbow. And he thought about heroes.

"No, sir," he said at last. "I don't think you were right to do that. I don't think you were right to do things that way at all."

"Oh," Mr. Thwaite said. "Well, I'm sorry you think that. Obviously, there's not much I can do to stop you going back to the guild and-"

"The way *I* think you ought to do it is this…" Emsley began.

The bar wasn't a very nice one. Deliberately so, it must be said, rather than merely as the result of being taken over by a brewery. So deliberately so, in fact, that it had recently only failed to win the title of "scummiest bar in the kingdom" because the judges of the competition hadn't made it out alive to deliver their verdict.

It was the sort of bar that had denizens, rather than patrons. They were currently clustered around a dagger stuck into the wall in a way that would probably have solved half the crimes in the city had eye witnesses been there to conduct identifications at the time. Daggers stuck into the wall were a surprisingly rare occurrence in this bar, if only because their owners could generally think of better uses for them, but they at least knew what one meant when it was pinning a piece of paper in place.

"'s a map," one of the black clad throng declared. By the standards of most of the crowd, it made him practically a thinker.

"So?" a passing dark elf demanded, sparking a brief brawl. It was the kind of pub where it never took much. When the bodies were cleared away, the intellectual continued.

"So it says there's treasure is underneath the spot marked X."

An orc leaned forward, lifting up the map. "No, there isn't."

Somebody carefully explained the concept of a map to him. Several of the others listened in discretely. Or at least as discretely as they could while making plans to hurry off in that direction as soon as possible—which wasn't very discretely at all, given the sudden rush for the door.

At the bar, a black-cloaked figure ordered another beer. Emsley thought he'd earned it. Now, he just had to hope that Mr. Thwaite's map in one of the more heroic inns would do its job at approximately the same time. After all, the maps had promised both sides adventure and treasure, and if the opposition didn’t show up, well, Emsley wasn’t going to go around producing maps that weren’t accurate, was he? Especially not now that he was a full cartographer.

I Have a Cunning...

Archibald Kilgaard Banstrom didn't look much like an evil mastermind as he sat in the middle of his spacious workshop. He hardly ever wore black, suspected that tight spandex would make him look like some sort of sausage, and generally favored thick spectacles over a suitably disguising mask. In fact, he looked more like the sort of man whose most villainous activity was probably keeping a train set and insisting on it being referred to as a model railway at all times. Though there are of course some who would say that was villainous enough.

The lack of the traditional costume can be explained by the fact that Archibald was not, strictly speaking, an evil mastermind. Rather, he was the man that evil masterminds went to once they found out that they couldn't quite live up to the second half of the job description. It had come as a revelation to Archibald that people in silly costumes frequently had money, and that they were willing to spend large amounts of it to have someone else come up with the evil plan—particularly if said plan involved death-rays, giant robots, or hideously convoluted schemes to conquer the known universe.

Currently, Archibald was drawing.

"Katie?" he called out after a minute. "How many barrels do you think a rotating-laser-of-doom should have?"

“I don’t know,” his niece yelled back, from somewhere behind a collection of killer-robot parts. “Maybe six? Anyway, why am I stuck making coffee?”

“It’s your turn.”

Katie huffed and picked her way out from the workshop’s little kitchen area, holding two steaming mugs. She did look a bit like an evil mastermind, at least of the sort inclined to wander around wearing too much leather and locking up handsome heroes for later—although the odds of one of those ever making coffee were probably pretty remote. Today things weren’t quite that bad, although the thigh-high boots really didn’t go with the jeans and t-shirt.

Archibald resolved to have a word with her at some point—not that Katie would listen. At eighteen, she was old enough to make up her own mind, and she had apparently decided to do so at every opportunity. Her parents worried constantly as a result, occasionally ringing Archibald to let him know, presumably on the theory that worry worked better if it was spread around. They’d only accepted her working for him before university on the basis that designing fiendish plans for world domination kept her out of trouble.

“Are you sure about this whole laser-of-doom thing?” Katie set down Archibald’s coffee. He carefully moved it so it wasn’t sitting on the plan he was working on.

“What’s wrong with it?”

“Nothing. It’s just…”

Archibald raised an expectant eyebrow.

"The whole evil ray-gun thing is just so last season," Katie said. "What we really need now is-"

Archibald didn't get to hear his niece's opinion on what was in fashion—partly because he wasn't really listening, having already ordered several of the parts for the laser-of-doom. Mostly though, it was because someone chose that moment to kick the door down.

"Hold there, evildoers! Or should I say, 'freeze'?"

The Amazing Ice-o stepped through the ruins of the door and threw a blast of cold towards the ceiling as a warning shot. Snowflakes drifted down, matching the silver ones on his otherwise pale blue spandex. Ice-o did his best to fix the two evildoers with what he hoped was a menacing gaze.

It didn't seem to work.

"Well, you could say freeze," the young woman said. Her tone made it clear that Ice-o was about the stupidest looking thing she'd seen. "But that would make you seem like even more of an idiot than you already are, and I'm not sure the fabric of the universe could take something so apparently impossible."

"Did you even try the door handle?" the man added. "I'm fairly sure it was unlocked, you see. It generally-"

"Shut up!" Ice-o threw another blast of cold—this one hitting the cup in the young woman's hand.

"Hey! That's my coffee!"

"It will be more than that in a minute," Ice-o warned, as threateningly as he could manage. The young woman ignored him.

"Look, Uncle Archie… it's gone all icy."

"For I am Ice-o!" Ice-o declaimed. He'd heard that declaiming things properly was half the battle with villains. If you declaim sufficiently dramatically, most of them would fold up without a fight. "Here to put a stop to your reign of terror!"

"Just like a coffee flavored popsicle. I mean, how am I supposed to drink the thing now?"

"I said shut up!" Ice-o froze the ground at the young woman's feet. She took a step, discovered that high heeled boots and ice didn't mix, and found herself sitting rather abruptly.

"Now that was uncalled for."

The balding man half rose before appearing to decide better and sitting back down again. "Katie has done nothing to deserve that sort of treatment."

"I'll be the judge of that!" Ice-o grabbed the man, nearly lifting him from his feet. "I've heard what you do here—making evil plans, plotting… Well, I'm here to put a stop to it the hard way!"

"I'm sure there's been a misunderstanding."

"Yeah, right." Ice-o raised one blue gloved fist. "Prepare for pain, evil-"

A coffee mug makes a decent blunt instrument at the best of times. Filled with frozen coffee, Katie's was enough to send the would-be superhero sliding into blissful unconsciousness. Archibald gave his niece a pained look.

"I do hope you haven't killed him. There's always so much trouble when that sort of thing happens."

"Fat chance. He's probably got the thickest skull this side of an elephant, given how little brain there is in there."

Archibald felt that was probably slightly unfair, but he wasn't in the mood to point it out.

"I suppose we'd best restrain him, so that he doesn't do anything foolish when he wakes up."

Katie did that, tying the young man to a chair with a casual flair that suggested Archibald really needed to have that talk with her. Particularly since she then hefted the ray gun from a prototype killer robot. She must have seen Archibald's expression, because she shrugged.

"Relax, it's not like it works or any… oh, sorry."

Archibald ducked. Katie put the weapon down very carefully, right around the moment a groan announced that their guest was coming round. Possibly, Archibald thought, he was revived by the scent of scorched plans. He stepped over to the bound superhero.

"Now, how many fingers am I holding up?"

"I'm telling you nothing! Not even if you torture me. Not if you pour red-hot lead in my boots. Not even if you put me in, like, a giant hamster ball full of spikes and set it rolling. Not if you-"

Archibald held up a hand.

"If you're going to continue, would you mind if my niece made notes? I quite liked the hamster ball thing. Possibly, we could find a use for it."

That got a sullen expression.

Archibald sighed.

"Look, what's your name?"

"I am the Amazing Ice-o!"

"It makes you sound like a type of anti-freeze," Katie said from the side. Archibald gave her a pointed look. "Well, it does!"

Ice-o squirmed in his bonds.

"You won't be saying that once I've… bloody hell, who tied these knots? They're going to take ages."

"Me again." Katie gave him a cheery wave. Archibald decided it was time to intervene.

"I was thinking of your real name. I bet your mother doesn't call you Ice-o."

The superhero muttered something.

"I'm sorry… I can't hear you."

"I said she calls me Wilbert. I prefer Will… or Ice-o."

Archibald nodded.

"Will it is. Well, Will, you're quite new to the superhero game, aren't you? It's probably only been a month or two since you were, let's see, bitten by a radioactive penguin or something…"

"How did you know that?" Will demanded. "I never tell anyone that!"

Katie actually laughed at that. Though in a much nicer way than Archibald expected.

"You really are new. It's always some radioactive animal, or a strange amulet, or some scientific accident. Here, let's take that silly mask off…"

"Hey!" Will tried to back away, which was a bit awkward since he was still tied up. Katie caught him before he fell. She peeled away the mask, revealing a young man who probably wasn't much older than she was.

"Much better."

The young man looked caught between fury at having his identity revealed and surprise at how pleasant Katie was suddenly being.

"Tell me, Will," Archibald decided not to wait to see which he settled on, "did a bunch of other heroes put you up to this?"

Will shook his head.

"I'm not naming names. I know what villains are like. You'll come up with something horrible, like… like heat-seeking exploding tennis balls, and send them after them!"

Archibald filed that one away for later, and he saw Katie do the same.

"How about if I tell you what happened?" Archibald said. "You arrived, all shiny and excited, and you found that horrible little bar where the others hang out…"

"You probably got stinking drunk," Katie added.

Will shook his head. "I did not. Well, not very."

"…and you started boasting that you were going to clean up the evil in this town," Archibald continued. "And they, being extremely helpful, pointed you in the direction of a little workshop at the heart of that evil, which comes up with all the evil plans anyone could ever want at reasonable rates."

Will thought for a moment, then nodded. Archibald sat back down.

"I'd like you to consider something. Why do most villains fail?"

Archibald waited while Will thought. And waited. And…

"Can I help?" Katie continued without waiting for an answer. "It's because there's always a flaw in their evil plan, which is that things are so complicated that they can't make them work. I mean, if you want huge amounts of money, why mess around with giant robots that conveniently miss innocent bystanders when they fire their weapons? Why not start a pyramid scheme?"

Archibald was glad that Will actually thought about it.

"So what you're saying," the young man said at last, "is that you actually make the villains less efficient?"

Archibald nodded.

"So inefficient that they hardly hurt anyone?"

Another nod.

"But that can't be right. Wouldn't they find out? Would they come here for revenge?"

"Oh, they break the door down pretty regularly," Archibald said. He saw Will wince. "The thing is, they expect things to go wrong. All part of being a super-villain, really. And if they're not reasonable, well…" he pressed a button hidden on the work stool. Assorted spare parts stopped looking like failures and started looking rather more like weapons. Most of them were pointing at Will, who gulped.

"I think… I think I should probably be going."

Katie untied him, and he made for the door. Archibald couldn't help but notice that she went with him. He raised an eyebrow as Katie returned.

"Get his phone number, did you?"

"What? He was sweet. Well… sort of. You could have told him that those guns were just special effects, Uncle Archie."

Archibald shook his head.

"It helped him learn his lesson."

"And me mine, no doubt." Katie smirked at his expression. "What, you thought I didn't know mum and dad had asked you to talk with me?"

"Well," Archibald admitted, "they are a bit worried."

"Relax, I'm not going to become a super-villain—not after working here. Super-villains are idiots."

Archibald let out a breath he didn't know he'd been holding. He started to straighten his plans. Naturally, Katie timed the next part for the moment he was picking his coffee up, ensuring he spilled the maximum amount.

"I'm going to go to business school instead."

Archibald suspected that it was really time for that talk.

Middle

"Stupid thing!"

Reg hadn't had cause to tackle young women around the waist in the past, but he felt that people should always be open to new things. Consequently, he and Cindy hit the floor together almost a whole second before the universe he and Alf had been working on shot through the space Cindy's head had just occupied. It ricocheted off the wall of the shed with a crash, got tangled in one of those lengths of old hosepipes that always turns up in sheds, and spun its way down under the workbench.

Reg caught his breath and struggled back to his feet, before thinking better of it and sitting down on an upturned coal bucket. "You know, my memory must be playing tricks in my old age, because I could have sworn that I said not to hit it with a big hammer."

"Well, I thought you weren't serious," Cindy replied, standing up too. "Besides, it just seemed like a hitting things with big hammers kind of moment."

"Well, I suppose at least you're learning something about proper, hands-on engineering," Reg allowed, and he had to admit he was mildly impressed. It had taken him almost a month to get the hang of the Big Hammers Principle—although the thing about it was that it was one of those principles where you had to also know when *not* to use it.

“There has to be something we can do,” Cindy said. It would probably have been less irritating if it hadn’t been the seventh time she’d said it in half an hour.

Reg shrugged. “I don’t see why,” he pointed out. “There’s quite often nothing you can do about things in this world. Take cabbage soup, for example.”

“Cabbage soup?” Cindy repeated.

“Every Saturday for lunchtime, my Vera makes cabbage soup for us. I’ve tried telling her that I don’t like it. I’ve tried pointing out that *she* doesn’t like it. I’ve even tried hiding in the shed with Alf and pretending that the presence of brassica in any form will result in the spontaneous destruction of a number of star systems. It doesn’t make any difference. Some things you can’t change.”

“Not even if I fetch a sledgehammer?” Cindy asked.

Reg shook his head. “Not even then. The best thing we can do is… oh, bugger.”

“What?”

Reg nodded to the universe spinning under the workbench. It was revolving rather faster than it originally had been. More than that, faint orange lines were starting to appear on its surface.

“Cracking?” Cindy said. “I thought you’d welded it tight, Uncle Reg?”

“I had,” Reg said. “And don’t tell me I might have missed something in my old age. That’s not the welds. That’s just what happens if the weirdness level starts to get too high. Alf told me about it years back.”

"Van Phnaargal's Effect?" Cindy said. "But that's just theoretical. And it was only posited a few months ago. I read the paper."

"Really?" Reg shrugged again. "Well, I guess it sometimes takes those physicist types a while to catch up."

Cindy wasn't sure whether he was serious or not.

"Of course," Reg said, "the real problem comes if the cracking gets bad enough for the structural integrity to go. If that happens, we have a universe trying to unfold in a space the size of a shed, leading to… well-"

"The instant destruction of the world as we know it?" Cindy asked.

"Oh, nothing like that," Reg assured her. "It probably wouldn't blow up anything much bigger than the county."

That was not, as far as Cindy could tell, much of an improvement. At least, not unless they could get on a bus really soon.

"Still," Reg said, "look on the bright side. At least if we get blown up, your aunt won't be able to say anything about it to either of us."

It was a bright side, just not one that anyone would be choosing in the near future to light their way to bed. What they needed was a plan. Something that would stop all this and simultaneously make things so that Aunty Vera wouldn't be annoyed with either of them, but without reducing them to mere stains on the paintwork. It would, in short, have to be a very *good* plan.

"Uncle Reg?"

"Yes, love?"

"If there are cracks in the universe, doesn't that mean that we can get stuff inside now? I mean, we could get in enough to engage the fail safes, couldn't we?"

Reg considered that. He tried to think of all the grounds on which he could tell his niece not to be daft. There were a few. They included such things as the possibility of her losing rather more than a layer of skin off her hands this time. Unfortunately, in the 'pros' column, were the words 'it will blow up if you don't.' Put like that, there weren't many options.

"Oh, all right, but I'm doing it. Pass me that bit of wire over there, would you?"

It took him three goes and quite a lot of swearing to get the wire hooked through one of the opening cracks. Now, he just had to edge it into place, short the safety controls, and hope that did the trick. Of course, to do that, he was going to have to *find* the safety controls, and it occurred to Reg that trying to find something like that, using nothing more than the feeling along one piece of wire, was pushing things out of the realms of engineering and into the miraculous. Still, given his line of work, that wasn't necessarily such a problem.

"Cindy, there's an endoscope on the bench. Don't ask why. Just get it in there to have a look, all right."

Cindy nodded, and once more, Reg had to admire the girl's talent. It only took her one go to get the thing in. She put her eye to it.

"Stars, stars, something to do with some intergalactic delivery company, blackness of space. Hang on, I've got it. You need to be a bit to your left. No, your other left. It's, well, it looks like about three light years from here."

Reg swore. He hated fiddly jobs. Now, if he could just get it into the right spot…

"There," Cindy said, "I think you've snagged it."

"Good, now I've just got to keep things steady long enough to… ow!"

At almost exactly the same moment as Reg dropped his bit of wire, Cindy lost her grip on the endoscope, leaving it sticking out of the universe as it spun, causing the thing to start a sedately lopsided wobble around the floor. Damn it, he should have known better than to think that just because he got something inside, the thing was going to hold still.

Worse, snagging it like that seemed to have done something to the universe. The cracks on it were still there, but now they were harder to spot, because the whole thing was glowing an angry orange. Tentatively, Reg reached out with another bit of wire. The end melted before it could even touch the thing. That was probably a bad sign.

Cindy echoed that thought. "There must be a build-up of some kind of energy in there, and it's not siphoning off into the usual stuff."

"Things found down the back of sofas and mindless TV soaps, you mean?" Reg scratched his head. It was technically possible for a universe to exist without those things, though he'd never seen one. Even the one he and Alf had created as somewhere for all the odd socks in the world to go still got re-runs of *Dynasty*. "Well, that's weird."

Reg wasn't usually a man to say that things were getting weird. He was, after all, a man who had once had to make half a solar system out of paper mache because they were in a hurry and Alf didn't have time to go to the wholesaler's. If you started saying that things were weird in his job, you would never stop.

"It's going to get weirder," Cindy pointed out. "Weirder and weirder until… kablooie."

Well, at least Reg had learned something today—specifically that there were people in the world who would actually say the word "kablooie." You lived and learned—at least until the thing exploded, of course.

Cindy, meanwhile, had started to pace around the interior of the shed keeping her eye on the universe, which had gone from orange to a bright yellow. "What do we do, Uncle Reg? What do we *do*?"

Reg wanted to say something about starting by being calm, but frankly, he wasn't feeling all that calm himself at that point.

"I think," he said, "that we start by doing the obvious thing."

"What's the obvious thing?" Cindy demanded.

By way of an answer, Reg stood up, picked up the coal bucket, and maneuvered it carefully into place over the universe. Underneath it, the thing spun faster still.

"I think it's time I made a few phone calls," he said.

Trust

At the center of his office, among the charts and the computers, the equations and the precisely placed empty coffee cups, Arvind the Reckoner stood as still as he possibly could. It was all he could think of to do, under the circumstances. True, the possible futures probably weren't *that* sensitive, but you never knew—except, of course, that Arvind *did* know, and that was the problem.

He could see the futures spreading out in clear, perfectly-calculated probabilities. Ordinarily, that wasn't a problem. He'd built a whole business on it, after all—a few simple problems sorted out for clients who needed to know what to do for the effects they wanted and who were prepared to pay plenty for the privilege. It was just a question of following a few pathways through, understanding what was needed, and pinning them down to definite end points.

Now, though, possibilities spun around Arvind's head like angry bees, weaving through one another in complex patterns of factors and causes until even he couldn't see where they led. No, that wasn't true. He could see the end points clearly enough, just as he could see the starts, leading back to this room, to this point. It was just… there was so much in between—so very much.

"Arvind, are you there?"

Arvind had foreseen the possibility that his secretary Megan would show up for work early, but he had been so busy with trying to make sense of things that he hadn't bothered to take the most basic of precautions, like locking the door. As such, the young, blonde haired woman wandered straight in, totally ruining Arvind's concentration.

"Arvind, what are you… oh, I'm sorry, you're in the middle of a calculation, aren't you?"

Megan always seemed so fascinated by Arvind's calculations. At least, she found all kinds of excuses to be in his office. Presumably, she eventually intended to get into advanced probability work herself, although Arvind didn't think that was very likely, based on what he knew of her mathematical abilities. And when he didn't think something was very likely, it *really* wasn't very likely.

"Arvind," Megan asked, "are you all right?"

"Please," he said, "I'm trying to concentrate. There are so many things to think about…"

"Oh, my sister was like that with her wedding," Megan bubbled. "She had, like, a million things to do at once. There was the dress, and the cake, and… and I'll shut up now, shall I? Would you like some more coffee? Of course you would. You always do."

Arvind couldn't answer for a moment as more possibilities swamped him. He could have coffee or not have coffee. He could have it with sugar or with cream… a latte, or cappuccino, or espresso… And for all he knew right now, that could be the decision that made the difference between a worldwide catastrophe and world peace. Or it could just be a cup of coffee. So he remained still—except that he couldn't remain still forever. He needed…

"Help," he croaked as Megan reached the door. She turned back. "Help. I can't… there are too many paths."

She hurried back. "Come on," she said kindly. "Come and sit down."

"But even sitting down might be enough to affect an outcome. What if-"

"I thought there wasn't any 'what if' with you," Megan pointed out. "I thought you *knew* what would happen."

"Not now," Arvind replied. "Not since taking on that job for the Department of Chaos Theory over at the university, and not since…"

Megan raised an eyebrow. "Yes?"

"Well, not since I tried to work out what you were doing here. I mean, you have a master's degree, so why would you be here, working as my secretary? And I tried to look at whether you would stay, and there just isn't enough information. So between that and the rest of it…"

"You quite literally don't know which way to turn," Megan finished for him. "Sit down, Arvind. Nothing bad will happen."

"You can't know that."

"Of course I can," Megan said. "I sit down all the time, and bad things hardly ever happen because of it."

"Inductive logic is inherently flawed though, so-"

"So just because I've never pushed you over for being so silly before, that doesn't mean I won't do it right now?"

Arvind took the hint and sat down. Nothing bad happened immediately, but since he couldn't see the full workings of the patterns, that didn't mean anything. Ten years from now, his choosing to sit down right now might mean the total destruction of the human race. It was impossible to be sure.

"Now," Megan said, "the second thing I want you to do is calm down. Can you do that?"

She was using her 'talking to the crazy person' voice. Arvind remembered it from the last time they'd tried to fill in his tax return together. He still thought that fractals had no place in finance.

"I don't know," Arvind admitted. "Nothing makes sense."

"It's all right," Megan assured him, "we'll work this out."

"But I *can't* work anything out. That's the point."

Megan sat there and looked at him for a while. "You said that this started after doing work for the Department of Chaos Theory?"

Arvind nodded. It had seemed like such a simple job. He just had to go in and evaluate a few of their funding applications to establish which ones would result in the best outcomes for the department. It had actually been fun, since the people there had seemed very interested in what he did.

"And let me guess," Megan said, "they wanted to have a long talk about the implications of their field for what you do, right? All about tiny changes and their potential knock on effects, water droplets rolling down slopes, butterflies with a complete disregard for other people's wellbeing, and things like that?"

A wave of fresh possibilities hit Arvind just at the thought of it, but he managed to nod.

Megan sighed. "Well, then, it sounds like you've been had."

Had? Arvind had almost as much trouble wrapping his mind around that concept as he did the probabilities. After all, he could see the consequences of actions laid out perfectly for him, so how could anyone hope to fool him. “I can’t be-”

“Tricked?” Megan laughed. It was quite a beautiful laugh. “Just because you can work things out, that doesn’t mean you know everything, Arvind. Believe me on that. And also believe me when I tell you that the university has just opened its own Department of Predictive Probability Extrapolation, whose members are normally carefully forbidden from going anywhere *near* the Chaos Theory mob.”

“So what… what do I do?” Arvind asked.

Megan shrugged. “I think we should start with an early lunch, don’t you? No, don’t answer that. I know you can’t decide. But I can, all right?”

It *was* all right. Megan took him down to the little café on the corner of the block that Arvind occasionally used to go to when he was a student. He’d spent hours then, watching people and working out what they would order before they did it. Working out the basics of the approach that would get him so far. He hadn’t been there in so long, mostly because he’d always been able to calculate that staying in the office was a more efficient use of his time. Now, coming back here, a wave of nostalgia hit him. It was almost powerful enough to wipe out the problems caused by all the choices on the menu.

Megan guided Arvind to a seat in the corner and ordered for them. Arvind briefly wondered what effect a chili dog and fries would have on his day, and he groaned as fresh futures spiraled off.

"The chili dogs here can take people that way sometimes," Megan said with a smile.

"Megan, this is serious. I can't see anything. I can't keep up with the calculations."

"Then don't," Megan suggested. "Just for now, don't calculate anything. Don't think about anything except what a nice lunch this is—which, admittedly, will need a certain amount of creative thinking on your part."

"But that's… it's like being blind, Meg. I mean, what if some vital decision shows up in the middle of lunch, and I don't spot it?"

Megan reached out to take his hand. "I know. You're just going to have to trust that it probably won't. Now eat your chili dog."

There was something in her tone that brooked no argument, so Arvind ate. It certainly took his mind off his other problems. Now he remembered why he had always ordered salad here as a student.

"Now focus," Megan said. "I need you to hear what I have to say. It doesn't matter that you can't track all the pathways out there, Arvind."

Arvind shook his head. "But it does. The Chaos Theory people specifically outlined the difficulties in tracking events when there are so many complex factors—any one of which could…" he stopped again and forced himself to take another bite of the chili dog.

"But they don't," Megan said. "Most of the time, they don't."

"But-"

"You can handle some of the pathways, right?" Megan asked.

Arvind nodded. "The simpler ones, but I see that there are so many factors now. So many more things that could change than I believed."

"Meaning that they're out of your control?" Megan suggested. "And, of course, you don't like things being out of control, except that sometimes, it's a good thing."

"Like when?" Arvind demanded. "When could it possibly be good for things to be out of control?"

Taking her cue, Megan kissed him. Arvind sat there for several seconds before he kissed her back. "I hope that answers the question about why I've been hanging around?"

Arvind nodded. "But it just makes things worse." He saw Megan's expression. "I'm sorry. That's not what I mean. You see, I can't even think of the right thing to say."

Megan smiled briefly. "You were never much good at that. Why does it make things worse then?"

"Because it was a cause I hadn't even considered, and if one of those can be around, why not others? Who's to say that every analysis I do won't be-"

Megan shut him up with another kiss.

"That's not an answer," Arvind insisted.

"It is an answer, actually." Megan took his hand. "I did it, and I didn't know what would happen. But nothing bad happened, did it?"

"Well… no. It was… nice."

Megan nodded. "Exactly. And would you mind pausing slightly less the next time I ask you something like that?"

"Sorry," Arvind said, then shook his head. "You've got me doing it again."

"Listen," Megan explained. "My point isn't that hard to understand, is it? You think that you can't tell what's going on, what's going to happen?"

"That's because I can't!"

"Welcome to how everyone else feels. And you know how we get through it? By trusting. By trusting that even though we don't know for certain, things will probably be all right."

"But my job," Arvind insisted. "How can I do that if I can't calculate?"

Megan took a bite of her chili dog. She gave every indication of enjoying it. Arvind certainly hadn't guessed that one. "You *can* calculate—at least in the same terms you have been, and probably in more detail than everyone else."

"But there's always more detail."

"Most of which is completely stupid," Megan pointed out. "You know what really happens when a butterfly flaps its wings in the Amazon. It gets eaten by something bigger."

"I'm not sure that 'completely stupid' represents a valid scientific category," Arvind tried.

"Really? Because most scientists of my acquaintance are really quite good at it. They can't even spot, for example, when a girl would like to go out with them." Megan paused to let that sink in before continuing. "So now, you have a choice, Arvind. Are you going to say yes or no?"

"There's not enough data."

"Remember what I said before about trust. Yes or no, Arvind?"

Arvind thought. The pool of possibilities was still there floating around him. He couldn't trace them. He could see the general shape of something, but the details… he could never hope to pick apart all the details. So what should he do? What did he *want* to do?

"Yes."

Afterwards, when Arvind was safely back at the office, nursing a headache, Megan made a phone call to the local university's admin offices.

"Hi, Kelly."

"Hi, Sis."

"I just wanted to say thanks for that little favor. Those Chaos Theory guys would never have called in Arvind on their own."

"My pleasure," her sister said. "If there's ever anything else…"

"Well," Megan said, "there was one thing. You know how it's the university interdepartmental bowling next weekend?"

"Sure, I'm helping to arrange it."

Megan smiled to herself. "I thought you might be. I was just thinking that maybe you could make sure the Department of Predictive Probabilities draws the Chaos Theory guys in the first round. I'm sure they'd have *plenty* to talk about."

When she finally put down the phone, Megan smiled again. Arvind had asked her out, and the university's finest minds would soon be having a long chat about the impossibility of the prediction department doing its job, leaving Arvind on top of the prediction pile once more. Megan couldn't tell exactly what the future would hold, but she had enough of an idea for now. For the rest… well, she'd just have to trust.

The Midsummer Sessions

Doctor Yvette Zimmerman downed the last of her coffee, steeled herself for the day, and rang through to let Marcy know that she should allow the first clients through. It generally wasn't a good idea for a couples' counselor to leave clients alone together in the waiting area too long, after all—particularly not given the kind of damage some of her clients could do.

Oberon and Titania walked in, looking as impossibly beautiful as ever, which just went to show that looks didn't guarantee anything. They said hello, then sat as far from one another as they possibly could—Oberon on one of the comfortable chairs Yvette had paid so much for, and Titania on a leafy bower that just happened to appear as she sat down.

"Huh," Oberon said. "Showing off. And I thought that we weren't supposed to use magic here?"

That was Doctor Zimmerman's usual rule, but today, it seemed that there were more important things to consider. "Would you both like to tell me what's going on? I thought things were starting to go well with these sessions."

Titania looked up sharply. "He's an ass, that's what's wrong."

"Funny," Oberon shot back, "I thought that was something you liked in a man."

"You're never going to let that go, are you? Well, I don't see why I should put up with that kind of thing from you. I'm the queen of my own kingdom, you know, and I could perfectly easily get together an army of-"

"You still haven't told me what happened," Yvette pointed out. She didn't normally like interrupting clients, because she didn't want them to feel that their feelings weren't valued; but when armies were being brought into the mix, it was generally time to put a stop to things.

"He missed our anniversary," Titania explained, jabbing a finger towards Oberon. "You'd think Midsummer Day wouldn't be that hard to remember."

"I didn't forget," Oberon retorted, "I-"

"And then, when I sent Puck and the rest to find out what he was up to, do you know what they found? They found him giving love potions to mortal women… *again.*"

"And young men," Oberon put in.

"Is that supposed to make it *better*?" Titania demanded.

"You see," Oberon snapped, "she won't listen to me even when I try to tell her what's going on."

Yvette made what she hoped was a calming gesture. "Well, then, why don't you just say it? Just say, right now, what was actually happening."

"Well… it's a bit embarrassing."

"You see, I knew-"

"Titania," Yvette sighed, "I'm sure we've spoken before about not jumping to conclusions. Oberon?"

The king of the faeries looked a little uncomfortable. "I just wanted to try to recapture some of the magic. So I thought, maybe if I reminded Titania what it was like back then, it might be nice—you know, turning people into things, playing tricks, befuddling mortals with love potions the night before their weddings… We used to have such fun."

"Oh," Titania said, "that's actually kind of sweet."

"But then you had to go and ruin things by not trusting me," Oberon replied. "Oh, and sending all your flower fairies to steal the love potions from half the people. Do you have any idea of the trouble you've caused?"

Titania stood. "The trouble I've caused? How dare you? And you're shouting. You know we aren't allowed to shout in sessions." She looked over to Yvette. "Are we?"

"Well, not as such, but-"

"What, the way you aren't meant to use magic."

"Well-" Yvette tried again.

Titania rounded on her. "Oh, I should have known. You're just on his side, aren't you? You know, I've got a good mind to report you to your association, or at least to ensure that you spend the next few months hopping around as a frog. In fact…"

"Sit down."

Yvette didn't generally like raising her voice when it came to her clients. Raising your voice generally meant that you were getting caught up in the argument, not to mention completely failing to provide a calm, safe, therapeutic environment in which to work. On the other hand, her clients were occasionally very irritating indeed.

"Well, I should think-"

"And you can shut up, too, Oberon."

For several seconds, the two rulers of the fey sat there in silence.

"There," Yvette said, "that's better. Now, hopefully, we can all discuss this like grown-ups. The idea is to work through your problems, not just to argue with one another."

Titania and Oberon still didn't speak, but they did glare at each other.

"After all," Yvette pointed out, "it's not like the two of you can really get away from one another. I mean, with a couple with such deeply entrenched issues, I might normally suggest that you start thinking about whether you genuinely want to be together anymore."

The two rulers of the fey were quiet for another moment or two. In that time, Marcy came in with coffee for them both. They sipped it sullenly.

"Actually," Titania said, "I'm starting to think that maybe we *should* spend more time apart."

"And I don't get any say in this?" Oberon demanded.

Titania looked momentarily like she might come back with a scathing response, but then she just looked resigned. "Oberon, face it, we haven't cared about each other in years. We're just making one another unhappy."

"Excuse me," Yvette tried, but they ignored her.

Oberon nodded ruefully. “You’re right. I know you’re right. It’s just… what we used to have was so good.”

“Used to have,” Titania pointed out. “Things haven’t really been the same since we stopped having to talk to one another in iambic pentameter.”

“Excuse me-”

“Well, we could try that again, couldn’t we?” Oberon suggested. “Or maybe an open relationship.”

Titania sighed theatrically. “We both know our relationship has been pretty open for a long time. You think I ever really believed that you were merely dancing and frolicking with those fair maidens. I looked up what frolicking means, love.”

Oberon winced. “I-”

Yvette tried once more. “Excuse me.”

“And the rustic with the animal head wasn’t the only one either.”

Oberon seemed to deflate. “Oh.”

“So you see, we’re really better off without one another,” Titania said. “I know it might seem harsh. I think we’ll probably always feel something, but it’s really better if…”

“… if we get a divorce,” Oberon finished for her.

“No, it damn well isn’t!” Yvette said, standing.

“Sorry,” Titania said. “What was that?”

Yvette shook her head. “You don’t get to divorce, you royal idiots. You’re the personifications of the seasons.”

“I say,” Oberon said, “do you mind?”

“What I mean is that if you break up, there will be problems.”

"Worse problems than we've been having?" Titania asked. "Because you of all people should know how bad things have been. Honestly, Yvette, I would have thought that you, of all people would know that there comes a point when it is simply better to walk away."

"Generally, yes," Yvette said.

Titania and Oberon stood. Oberon spoke. "Well, you see how it is then. I'm glad you agree."

"I said 'generally'." Yvette moved to stand in front of the door. "By which I mean 'for those clients where a trial separation will not cause massively destructive climate change'. Not to mention the probable war between the different factions of the fey."

To their credit, the two rulers of the faerie world at least thought about it. Eventually though, Titania shook her head.

"Sorry," she said, "obviously in every breakup, there is going to be a certain amount of pain, but in this case, I really do think it's better than the arguments if we stay together."

"The world's grown up now," Oberon added. "It can probably deal with this much better now, and if it can't, well… I hate to sound harsh, but tough."

"And the war?" Yvette asked.

"Oh, I think we can get through this slightly more amicably than that," Titania suggested. "After all, we've had separate spheres for years."

"Well, maybe that's part of the problem," Yvette tried.

Titania reached out and picked her up easily, lifting her away from the door. "I know this must be hard for you, dear. It probably feels like you've failed or something, but let me assure you, you haven't."

"No," Oberon said. "Why, without you, I'm sure that we would have been stuck in an endless cycle of recriminations and badly rhyming badinage. Instead, we're going to be free to be the people we really want to… is it just me, or does that coffee have quite an aftertaste to it? Almost like…"

He collapsed into an enchanted sleep. A second later, Titania followed, and Yvette breathed a sigh of relief. That had been close. She carefully arranged the two of them to face one another when they woke, and then walked out into the reception area, where Marcy was waiting, perched on the edge of her desk.

"Did it go all right?" her secretary asked.

"Pretty much the way it always does with those two. Honestly, one of these days, I'm going to get through our weekly session without them almost making it to the door before the love potion kicks in."

"That's the price of working with faerie folk, I guess," Marcy suggested. "Still, it's worth it for what Robin Goodfellow and the rest pay us to keep them together—not to mention the whole world not being destroyed thing."

Yvette nodded. "True. Incidentally, was it just me, or did the stuff take slightly longer than usual to kick in today?"

"Well, um…"

Yvette raised an eyebrow. "This isn't for that bike courier who keeps stopping by, is it? Honey, you don't need a love potion for that one."

Marcy looked briefly embarrassed. "Sorry, it's just nice to be sure."

Yvette thought back to the couple currently sleeping it off on her floor, and what would happen if they ever got as far as the divorce lawyers. "Yes, I guess it is."

The Final

On the plain of Asgath, under the red twin suns, the armies of Light and Dark lined up, ready for what was to be the final battle. They were fairly easy to tell apart, even though Light had ditched its usual white surcoats in favor of an away strip of pastel blues and pinks. After all, when one side was populated by elves singing tra-la-la, and the other side mostly featured orcs who would never sing *anything* that didn't qualify as a drinking song, confusing the sides wasn't much of an issue.

The issue lay with what was currently between them. Not *everything* between them, it must be said. The commanders of Light and the overlords of Dark had no problem with the general sweep of the grassy plain, sitting between two ranges of hills quite neatly. No, that was perfect battle terrain, as far as they were concerned—just nice enough for letting the lads work up a good head of steam before they smashed into one another.

The problem was with the small square of picnic cloth situated almost exactly halfway between the two armies.

Maud and Ethel always enjoyed their little days out. They got a nice walk out in the fresh air, and they got to take a big hamper full of food, which Ethel always got through, despite her insistences that she was watching her figure. Maud was slightly more honest about it. After all, everyone else had stopped watching her figure twenty years previously, so why should she bother.

"Well, this is nice," Maud said.

"They say it might rain later though," Ethel put in.

"Well, that's not a problem. I brought the umbrellas, and I know you have your warm coat with you. You *always* have your warm coat with you."

Ethel shrugged. At her age, it took some time. "You never know when you might need a warm coat."

"Ethel, I think maybe sometimes you *do* know. I mean, you took your coat to that time in the desert."

"Well, it *might* have turned colder. Oh, look, there seem to be some people coming down."

There were, although Maud had to put her spectacles on before she could see them all properly. There were two parties, in fact—one from either side. From the Light side, there seemed to be a selection of paladins, accompanied by an elf lord or two. From the Dark side, there were a few types in spiky black armor, along with a goblin chieftain riding some kind of pony-sized wolf. From the looks of it, the two groups would arrive almost simultaneously.

They did. Two figures in full armor leaped down at almost exactly the same moment to demand that Maud and Ethel get out of the way. It made for quite a nice stereo effect, to Maud's ears, but still, there was such a thing as manners—for other people, at least.

"Now, didn't your parents ever teach you to take turns when speaking?" Maud demanded after a second or two of it.

"I had no parents," the one in the black armor with the spikes said. "I was born in the Pit of Doom, created from the purest flow of evil."

"That's nice, dear," Maud said, then nodded to the figure from the Light side, whose armor was rather shinier. "And just for that, your friend here can go first."

"We are not friends," the light armored one insisted.

"Well, that's a shame," Ethel put in. "Isn't it a shame, Maud, when people can't get on?"

"What's your name then?" Maud asked.

"Know that I am Dougal, paladin of Light. You may recognize me as the winner of last years 'maiden rescuing' championships."

"Strange," Ethel said, "you don't *look* worn out."

Maud gave her a pointed look.

"From carrying them away from danger, I meant. Who's the other one, then?"

"I am Foeslayer."

"Is that what your mother calls you, dear?" Maud asked.

"As I said before, I have no-"

"You know, he reminds me of my Brian," Ethel said. "Well, except for the armor and things."

Nobody pointed out that the armor was all anybody *could* see of Bri-Foeslayer, nor did anybody snigger towards the back. The spikes on his armor looked very sharp, after all. There was, however, a faint suggestion in the air that their spokesperson would henceforth be answering to a new name.

“Listen, ladies,” Dougal said. “There is a battle starting up here soon, and you are right in the middle of it.”

“Oh,” Ethel said with a certain amount of excitement. “You mean like one of those historical recreation things? Are you with the Sealed Knot, dear?”

“I’m with the Order of St. Opugnator, actually,” Dougal explained.

“And *I* am with the Dark Order of Absolute Doom,” the newly renamed Brian put in.

“Well,” Maud said, “I’m sure it’s nearly the same thing. Would either of you boys like a scone?”

“We wish to crush our enemies!” Brian roared.

“That’s nice, dear, although if you *could* refrain from shouting? And there’s to be no crushing while we’re eating, you understand? Good boy.”

Brian (who was by now wondering how he was going to explain the name back at the Pit) turned to his party of evil compatriots for support. Unfortunately, by that point, two of them were busily eating cupcakes, while the goblin chieftain was chatting with Ethel, who was stroking his wolf’s tummy, while commenting on what a big softy it was really. About the only thing to be said for it was that the party from the Light side seemed to be suffering the same treatment. Maud was busy pouring lemonade for one of the elf lords, while a couple of the paladins seemed to be sitting on their hands, having made a dive for the biscuits a little too quickly.

With a certain amount of reluctance, Brian sidled over to Dougal. "Is this your doing? Some ploy to stop your inevitable defeat at the hands of Darkness?"

"Me? I thought it was you."

"What are you two boys up to?" Maud asked. "Come over here and sit down. I'm sure I have some pictures of my grandchildren somewhere."

When the scouting parties were able to beat a retreat and head back to their respective sides, their commanders were not impressed by their underlings' inability to deal with two inconveniently placed old women. They pointed out that it would have been easy to simply remove them by force, but the men demurred. Those on the Light side pointed out that they couldn't very well go around harming old women, while those on the Dark said that they *had* to be on their side, or else how did you explain the slow torture of the grandchildren's pictures?

Because no one gets to be the leader of an army in the ultimate battle without a certain amount of firmness (not to mention tactical knowledge, the ability to inspire one's troops, and twenty ways to tell the press that the early season slump wasn't their fault), they ordered their underlings to go back and do it properly. They even threatened to behead those who failed. Sadly, that didn't seem to have the desired effect on morale. Apparently, there were scarier things in the world than a quick beheading. Actually, both leaders knew that perfectly well. It was just that neither had heard of any scarier things that happened to involve cupcakes.

Determined to put a stop to the foolishness, not to mention all too aware of the amount of overtime the troops were racking up while waiting for the order to charge, the leaders of the two sides then mounted their own steeds of choice (a unicorn for the leader of the Light, and for the chief overlord of Darkness, a skeletal dragon held together by evil sorcery and gaffer tape) to take care of the matter personally.

Twenty minutes later, they rode back to their respective sides, each pausing only briefly to ask the other if they were sure that the women didn't work for them. Sadly, it didn't seem that such an easy excuse for slaughter was going to present itself. So they waited, instead, and shouted at the first person to ask why they were waiting so loudly that no one else asked.

After the first five minutes, each wondered how long eating a few scones and admiring the scenery could take. After an hour, they contemplated sending down another party to ask, but they couldn't bring themselves to do it. After three hours, they realized that the old biddies were there for the duration, and they tried to pluck up the courage to shout "charge" anyway. Sadly, both suspected that at least some of their respective armies would have grandmothers, and besides, how would it look to the bards, going around doing that kind of thing? The wrong media coverage could totally ruin an army's post season.

So they kept waiting, and they pretended that it didn't bother them. The leader of the Light amused himself by practicing the harp, while the leader of the Dark tortured a few of his lowest minions (although given that the leader of the Light was only up to page three of "easy songs for little harpists," it is hard to say who caused more suffering). A few of their soldiers looked askance at such a blasé approach to winning the final battle, but as time wore on, they assumed that it must be some kind of cunning tactic that they simply hadn't been paying enough attention to back when they'd all been going over things with the chalk boards.

Eventually, with the light fading, the two leaders walked out to the front of their respective hordes. It really was now or never. Over the vast emptiness of the plains of Asgath, their eyes met, and barely, just barely, they both nodded. When they spoke, it was with one voice.

"Right, lads. That's it. We're going home."

A little further away on the plains, hidden behind a small rock, a watcher lowered a pair of binoculars and turned to his compatriot, who didn't look like anything very special. But that was all right, because neither did the first watcher. In fact, both had the kind of studied unremarkableness that was, in its way, quite remarkable.

"Looks like they're packing up, Tony."

"Looks like it, Franco. One no score draw, exactly as ordered."

Tony, the watcher who hadn't been watching, made a note on a clipboard. "And by my reckoning, that gives us a pretty good return, given the way the odds were getting at the end."

Franco nodded. "Sure. Should we go get the ladies yet?"

Tony considered it. On the one hand, they did have another battle to get to a couple of dimensions over, and their boss was not the kind of man who appreciated lateness. On the other, he knew as well as anyone what Maud and Ethel could be like if they tried to move them before they'd finished the hamper. Honestly, things had been a lot easier when they'd stuck to just rigging *sports.*

"I think we'll give it just another few minutes."

Trying to Get Out

Maggie was kind of an expert when it came to diets. She'd been on enough of them over the last couple of years, after all—all the famous ones: sticking to one kind of food or another, or swearing off carbs, or counting calories, or picking out options from a little guide book that told her what she could have… which never turned out to be what she actually wanted, come to think of it.

It wasn't that she was *fat* fat. She didn't make cars tilt to one side by getting in the passenger seat, or make small children stare, or anything. Most places, she might even have been called normal sized or curvaceous maybe. It was just that she had to go and act, and she had to go and turn out to have a bit of talent for it—enough that people occasionally asked her to audition now rather than waiting for her agent to very carefully ask them—enough that she generally got almost all the way through the process before someone asked if she would mind losing a few pounds for the role, just to fit in the director's vision of the role… and possibly the costumes.

Because Maggie was generally quite conscientious, she did her best every time. She had personal trainers and advice from diet gurus, all the usual kinds of thing, and generally she managed to drop a few pounds for the role. Never quite as many as the director would have liked, of course, and they never stayed off. It was never like Maggie was able to say goodbye to them permanently. It was more like they recognized that they were required to take a brief vacation, but then they came back happy, rested, and ready to resume the difficult work of sitting around Maggie's hips.

The trouble was, she wasn't sure she could keep doing that. After all, there was only so much running a girl could do, wasn't there? And getting down to almost what the studio had in mind wasn't going to cut it in the long run. Besides, Maggie was just starting to hit the stage in her career when people with cameras were starting to pay attention to her between jobs, and if she looked like some kind of elephant, then… well, what would that do?

She needed something more permanent, only cosmetic surgery didn't sound like too much fun, and everybody in the business had heard the stories about what could go wrong. There was the one about the actress who had come out looking like her face had just been inflated with a bicycle pump and the one about the surgeon who was sufficiently hung over from the night before not to notice that the plans for his work were upside down. Maggie wasn't going to go along with that kind of thing, even if her agent had dropped one or two hints.

So when a friend of hers (well, not a friend exactly... more like someone she'd met at a party) told Maggie that one of her friends had managed to lose thirty pounds like it was nothing, and keep it off, Maggie was willing to at least listen, even if she knew enough about diets by then to know that it never really worked like that. The friend of a friend didn't have many details beyond the name FGMEnterprises, but she took Maggie's number, and promised to get back to her with more.

This was how, just a couple of days later, Maggie came to be sitting in a nice, quiet place that looked like a private clinic, reading a magazine, while a little way away a receptionist conducted a long phone conversation with someone whom Maggie decided after a while was probably her boyfriend. She still wasn't entirely sure why she was there. After all, she'd tried looking up the place online, but it hadn't looked much like a diet clinic. There hadn't been all the usual marketing before and after photos for one thing. There hadn't been strings of glowing references. There hadn't been much of anything at all.

Actually, maybe that's what had convinced her to phone up and make an appointment when the friend of a friend had gotten back to her a day or so later. Maggie had come up with her own little rules about diets—the first one of which was that the more people that shouted about theirs, the less likely it was to actually do anything useful. Working by that rule, this one had to be something special.

Of course, the bit where she'd also asked a few discrete questions and found out who the friend of a friend was had helped. Maggie had seen the magazine pictures of her, and an editor friend of hers assured her that they really weren't airbrushed, which was saying a lot, given what they usually did to Maggie's photos on official shoots.

After a short wait, the receptionist indicated that Maggie could go through. How she knew that, since she still hadn't concluded her argument with her boyfriend, Maggie wasn't entirely sure. She went through anyway. The room she ended up in was quite small, with a mirror at one end, a desk at the other, and a very thin and well-dressed woman standing somewhere between the two.

"You must be Maggie," the woman said, extending a hand. "I'm Francesca. So, you want to lose a few pounds?"

"A few," Maggie admitted, "and someone said that you were the person to come to."

"Well, they're right. Although let's both be honest from the start, shall we? It's more than a few, isn't it?"

That struck Maggie as kind of a bitchy thing to say, but she let it slide. Presumably, diet experts were allowed to make comments about people's weight.

"I guess. Look, I just want to be sure that you can really help me. I mean, I've tried so many things."

Francesca reached out to pat her arm. "We all have. Believe it or not, there was a time when I was the same. I was overweight, and I was miserable, trying all sorts of things to be the person I wanted to be. I tried all the usual stuff before I finally found the one little thing I needed, and now it's like I'm someone else entirely."

"And what was that thing?" Maggie asked. "Your website is pretty vague, and I'm not going in for anything that involves surgery."

"Oh, I completely understand, and it's nothing like that at all, though we generally don't give out details to non-clients. All I can say is that it really does work like magic, and I'd be happy for you to talk to any of our clients to confirm that. You are serious about this, aren't you?"

Maggie explained that she was serious, and to demonstrate that seriousness, she even wrote Francesca a check when asked for an amount of money that couldn't really be anything else.

"So what is it?" Maggie asked at last. "What is this thing that works like magic?"

"Why, it's magic, of course."

"Magic." Maggie laughed. "That's great, but really, what are you going to do?"

Francesca walked over to her desk, where she took a long stick out of a drawer. Though possibly 'wand' might have been a more appropriate word. "I'm going to use magic on you, Maggie."

"Right. I think I'll be going now then... Oh, and don't try to cash that check."

There was a pencil sharpener sitting on Francesca's desk. She pointed her wand at it, and it became a toad, which, presumably in response to some kind of inner drive, wandered over to a pencil and tried to eat it.

Maggie stared at the toad for a while. Finally, with all the eloquence that her acting career to date could muster, she said, "Oh."

"Now," Francesca said, "shall we get on with it?"

"T-there's really such a thing as magic?" Maggie asked.

Francesca sighed. "Yes, dear, though if you're going to go through the whole denial phase, could you possibly do it quickly, I have another appointment at three o'clock."

"You know, you really aren't that nice."

Francesca shrugged. "I imagine it comes with what I am. And before you ask, no, I'm not a witch. I'm a fairy godmother. I used to be, anyway. I was always wandering around, squeezing my fat self down into kitchens to grant wishes, but then I thought… well, I'm not setting a very good example, going around telling girls that they look lovely enough for any handsome prince, while I was built like a sumo wrestler, so I took a few steps. And afterwards, I saw what a dead end the godmothering business was, when I could be out helping people who really need the assistance."

"And getting paid for it," Maggie put in.

Francesca beamed. "Exactly. Now, can we get on with it?"

"Get on with using magic on me?"

Francesca's smile slipped a little. "Three o'clock, remember?"

"Sorry, it's just… are you going to be doing the same thing you did to that pencil sharpener?"

Francesca shrugged. "Not unless you think that there are some big amphibian roles coming up."

"So, what are you going to do?" Maggie demanded. "I mean, are there going to be any side effects? Is it safe? Will I turn into a pumpkin at midnight?"

"That was just the once, and I don't know who told you about it, but-" Francesca obviously caught Maggie's expression because she stopped dead. "No," she promised, "nothing like that will happen. The magic is perfectly stable once I've done it. All that's left over is a thinner, happier you."

"So how-"

"Look, you've heard of the idea that inside every fat girl there is a thin girl dying to get out? Just think of me as the escape committee. Now, go over and stand by the mirror. It makes it easier."

Maggie did as she was told. After all, she had spent money on stupider diet ideas in her time—which probably said more about her than she liked, now that she thought about it. Even so, she stood nice and still while Francesca waved the wand at her. Nothing happened.

Then, just as Maggie was about to suggest that she would quite like her money back, something did. Specifically, she collapsed to her knees as agony ripped through her. It genuinely felt as though someone was ripping her guts out with a giant spoon—except that there didn't seem to be any spoons in evidence.

She was just about to scream at the other woman about her not having said anything about it hurting, or at least just scream, when hands helped her back to her feet. They looked like quite familiar hands, as it happened. More than that, the rest of the person they were attached to was quite familiar too.

"You're me," Maggie said.

"Or your me," the other her said. "Only fat, obviously."

That was a hurtful way to put it, even if the other her did look like she had just stepped off a catwalk.

"Meet your inner you, Maggie. The one you see in the mirror. The one who just needed a little help getting out."

Maggie looked at the other her for several seconds in pure amazement. Then one obvious problem struck her. "But this way, there are two of me. I mean, she looks great, but I'm still me. I'm still here."

"Yes," the other her said, with a smile that was far from friendly, "that is a problem, isn't it?"

Maggie realized then that the other hers arms were still around her, and they were lifting. She glanced back. Behind her, the mirror no longer seemed to have any glass in it. Instead, it was more like a giant black hole.

"The problem with releasing the self that you really want to be," Francesca observed, "is that, then, there's this horrible, useless lump left over. We can't have that, can we?"

"Help!" Maggie bleated. She turned to her other self. "You can't do this. I'm you!"

Francesca laughed, perching lightly on the desk. "I don't see why that should make a difference. I got rid of me, after all. And you have to remember the one fundamental rule when dealing with any fairy magic that leads to there being two of you."

"What's that?" Maggie demanded.

"Why, one of you has to be the evil twin, of course." She hopped off the desk and went over to help the thinner Maggie with the lifting. Just before they threw Maggie into the darkness of the mirror, Francesca laughed. "On the whole, I think we have the better end of the deal, don't you?"

The High Life

Claire had her moment of inspiration waiting for a plane, when the check in girl accidentally upgraded her ticket to first class, and she got to sit in the first-class lounge, sipping champagne while enjoying a shiatsu massage. She hadn't had a shiatsu massage before, but it was obviously worth more than the nothing she was paying for it.

She said as much to the woman sitting next to her, who suggested that the massages given by her personal massage therapist were far superior and that should take the time to come over and try it, if they were going the same way. Claire agreed that they should, and by the time their plane landed in New York, Cynthia, who was the woman in question, had invited her to stay for a few days.

Maybe that would have been it, and Claire would have gone home embarrassed or broke by the end, but she quickly found that things didn't work like that. When they went shopping, Cynthia was as generous as only someone with no real grasp of money could be, while stores were happy to lend things to such distinguished guests for the party Cynthia that had planned back at her home.

The party was probably where things snowballed, because that was where Claire met a movie producer by the name of Andre, who was apparently so taken with the idea of a beautiful young woman who neither wanted an acting role from him nor wanted him to read her script that he invited her to stay on his yacht down in Florida. He had to go away for a few days to film after that, but he left Claire in the capable hands of his sister, who in turn introduced her to this fashion designer friend of hers, who passed her on to a business magnate from Austin.

It was a bit like being the class pet back in kindergarten. Claire would stay a couple of days, or a couple of months, with someone, they would know someone else who would simply *love* to meet her, and Claire would end up staying in their guest house, or spare room, or country lodge. And as the guest, *obviously,* she wouldn't pay for things. No, it was just accepted that when it became her turn to put other people up in her mansion, she would show the same level of hospitality.

Not that she ever said she had a mansion—people just assumed. After all, if she was hanging around with these people, she *had* to have a mansion, didn't she? Everyone except Claire seemed to think that, and after the first week or two, it was simply easier not to correct them. Besides, most people were too busy talking about themselves to ask, and Claire encouraged them, which got her a reputation for being a good listener. Particularly since she wasn't someone to go running to the gossip magazines with things.

She got a reputation as an elegant dresser, too. Partly, that was because people lent her so many clothes, and partly, it was simply because she'd had years of rooting around in charity stores for necessities. So when things, like retro and shabby-chic, had a phase of being in fashion again, she was ahead of the wave. She even got a little work modeling on the back of it, though Claire had a hard time believing that was real. It didn't net her superstar money, but it got her invited to more parties. It also got her some interest from an agent named Keith. More importantly, it kept her moving.

Keeping moving was the main thing. Claire saw more of the world in the next year or two than she had in the rest of her life, because she never dared to stop. If she stopped, it might end, and she wasn't sure she was ready for it to end—even though she still wasn't quite sure what "it" was. So she followed a minor rock guitarist around on tour, hopped off to stay on a private island, and flatly refused to settle down with the millionaire who offered to marry her. Claire wasn't that kind of girl, so she went off to do some promotional work for a small charity instead. Why a charity would want her, when they could have had someone famous, Claire didn't know.

Things went reasonably well for a while. She was never the girl in the center of the pictures in the gossip magazines, but frankly, Claire had never wanted to be, so that was all right. She drifted around, following the routes that all the famous heiresses had before her, and because everyone assumed that she was one, they didn't ask anything of her besides her presence.

The first problem came when a couple of reporters started to ask who she was. Claire hadn't had that before. People had always just assumed that the people she was with knew, and so they should too. It would have been embarrassing to ask who Claire was, because that would have been admitting ignorance on a topic where clearly everyone else was an expert, or thought they were. Claire had heard a few rumors about herself since she started travelling. She'd even started a couple; they weren't true.

The trouble was that the reporters weren't satisfied with the rumors. They wanted in-depth interviews, and when Claire wouldn't give them, they asked their question openly. They demanded to know, in print, who Claire was. For not quite a week, people she had met, or stayed with, defended her, saying that it was a stupid question. After that though, they sat down and realized that it was a stupid question to which they did not know the answer, so they started to ask it too.

Perhaps it was one of those who engaged the private investigator, although it was certainly the reporters who got the results of his work. They were the ones who explained in some detail how Claire was just a poor girl from a poorer town, and they included pictures of her parents' house to prove it. They were the ones who sat on the doorstep of the producer with whom she was currently staying, demanding the truth from her until she couldn't put it off.

So she gave a press conference, or at least walked out onto the lawn with the few things she actually owned in a hold all. There, Claire carefully explained everything that had happened over the past couple of years. She said she was sorry if she had hurt anyone. She even cried at one point. Then she walked as far as the bus station and used the little cash she had to buy a ticket back to the family home.

By the time Claire got there, people were already saying that she ought to be prosecuted; people she hadn't met since school had come out to say how disappointed they were in her; and one minister had said that she was clearly a very misguided young woman who had put material things before anything else. Over the next couple of days, most of the people she'd stayed with gave press conferences, one by one, saying how shocked they were by the whole thing, how betrayed they felt, and that incidentally, they had a new album coming out Monday.

By the end of the week, Claire barely dared to show her face outside. No one had arrested her so far, but that was apparently only because she technically hadn't done anything wrong, and that never seemed like a good enough reason to the news people. So they settled for making her the most hated person they could for a week instead. A couple of people she'd met mentioned that she'd actually seemed perfectly nice, but they didn't get much air time.

So when she woke a morning or two later to find Keith, the agent who had wanted to work with her, banging on the front door, Claire almost hid under the bed. After all, he would probably only want to shout at her, or tell her he was pressing charges, or something. But he kept knocking, and eventually Claire had to answer, just to make him go away. He pushed past her and into the hall.

"Whatever it is," Claire said, "I don't have anything for you. I had a lot of fun, but I'm sorry if you feel I fooled you or anything."

"Sorry?" Keith said. "Why should you be sorry? Come on, we're going to go to breakfast."

Claire shook her head. "Sorry. I can't afford it, and I'm not getting anyone else to pay for things—not now."

"Can't afford it?" Keith laughed. "Girl, you haven't been paying attention…"

"I have. People hate me. I'm broke, and if I'm lucky, I might just manage to stay out of jail."

Keith shook his head. "They love you enough that the studios are willing to pay for the story. Then there's the book deal and the appearances. Putting one over on people like that? It's great!"

"But why would people want anything like that?" Claire asked. "Everyone I've ever met hates me."

"Oh, ignore them," Keith suggested. "When it's time for the premiere, half of them will come out and say that it was great fun and that they've learned an important life lesson."

"About not judging a book by its cover?"

Keith shrugged. "Something like that. Who cares? I'm going to make you a very rich woman."

"Rich?" Claire repeated. But she knew better than to ask things like that. Rich was relative. Even so, she briefly wondered what the millionaire lifestyle might be like with actual money. Might it not be better to say no? To go and live a normal life? Maybe to do something that was of some actual use?

On the other hand, why not?

Hunted

There was one thing Eleanor had found since dating Norman: she had come to own far more practical clothes than she ever had before—clothes she didn't mind getting covered in mud, primarily. There always seemed to be such a lot of mud, when it came to Norman. Today's mud was in a ditch by some trees on the edge of a rather larger patch of mud that qualified as farmland because it happened to have potatoes in it somewhere. According to Norman, they weren't even organic potatoes, though Eleanor had found herself wondering at several points over the last hour or so exactly how potatoes could qualify as inorganic—even when subjected to her idea of cooking.

"Are you sure we're in the right place?" Eleanor asked.

Norman put a finger to his lips. "Shh, they might hear you. You wouldn't want all this to be for nothing, would you?"

"All this" had included getting up at what Eleanor believed to be a totally unreasonable hour of the morning, packing up enough fair-trade coffee and vegan sandwiches to feed most of the starving children in Africa, and then going out to sit a ditch, waiting for the sound of hounds and horses. It was the sort of "all this" that came about mostly because Norman was so passionate about what he did, and because Eleanor was passionate about Norman. At least, she assumed that she was. She wouldn't live with him if she weren't, after all. And if occasional mornings spent in ditches were part of the deal, well… that was simply that.

"Just remind me," she said, "of exactly what we're going to do."

"It's very simple," Norman shot back, in the tones of someone who couldn't believe that simplicity wasn't obvious to everyone. "My friend Barry said his friend Irving saw a hunt out this way, so we're going to wait for them, and when they come past, on the trail of some poor, defenseless animal, we sabotage them. Easy."

"Easy," Eleanor agreed. She wondered if it was all right to ask exactly how someone went about sabotaging a hunt in full flow. She suspected, however, that it was one of those questions to which everyone was meant to know the answer, like why exactly anything with a brand name on it was inherently evil. Norman had struggled for quite some time to answer that one. Still, Eleanor thought she had best say something "Um… this isn't going to get *violent,* is it?"

"Look, Eleanor," Norman said, "I'm starting to wonder if you have as much commitment to this as I do. I can still remember what happened at the demonstration, you know."

Eleanor sighed. He wasn't going to let that one go, was he? And all because she happened to remark to a couple of Norman's friends that maybe hitting policemen with placards wasn't necessarily the best way to get them to listen to what they were saying. How was she to know that wasn't the way things were done?

"I'm here, aren't I?" Eleanor said.

"It's not enough just to be here," Norman explained. "We have to make a difference. And that means doing whatever we can to ensure that these people stop. Sometimes, violence is the only language they understand, you know."

Eleanor wasn't sure she liked the sound of that, but Norman was the expert. He'd said as much several times.

"Look," Norman said, "keep quiet and follow my lead, okay? They'll probably be along in a minute."

In fact it was almost another hour before they heard the baying of hounds. In that time, Eleanor had had plenty of opportunities to reflect on the suitability of mud as a form of seating, wonder about whether anything could be worth this much effort, and decide that she was going to take a very long bath when they got home, despite Norman's usual warnings about the eventual risk of global water shortages. Even so, she didn't complain out loud. She would show Norman that she was every bit as committed to this as he was—probably.

As such, she waited while the hounds approached, accompanied by assorted sounds of bugles, people shouting, "tally ho!" and all the other things people did at times like that. Beside Eleanor, Norman readied an air horn and held one end of a piece of string. Something shot past. It was small and red, but to Eleanor's eyes, it didn't look much like a fox. If anything, it looked very much like a small man in a red hat with a beard that probably wasn't very long in objective terms, but on a man six inches high was long enough that he had to be careful not to trip as his legs blurred beneath him.

Eleanor considered asking Norman what was going on, but he had been quite clear that she shouldn't make a sound until it was time. Besides, for all she knew, small men in red hats were perfectly normal at times like this. She'd never been what you could call a country person. In any case, a couple of seconds later, it was quite hard to ask Norman anything much, because he was too busy running out from their hiding place shouting. He had his horn and his string, blaring the one and holding onto the end of the other.

It occurred to Eleanor that she ought to follow, and that she also ought to show some enthusiasm if she was going to impress Norman. As such, she leapt out from her hiding spot, shouting and waving her arms. She hadn't been told to wave her arms, but she felt it was probably in the spirit of things, and she hoped that Norman would appreciate the small show of initiative in the name of the cause.

Eleanor shouted and waved her arms with such enthusiasm, in fact, that for a couple of seconds she didn't notice that Norman was no longer doing it. Only when she saw him standing there staring open mouthed did she look around and take in the hunt she was trying to sabotage properly.

The horses were… well, some of them were huge black things, with small gouts of flames coming from their nostrils, while others were greenish, with seaweed hanging from their manes, and still more were pure white, with what looked very much like horns sticking out of the middle of their heads. The dogs with them were just as… varied, with some of them being huge and orange eyed, while others looked more like wolves, and a couple were things that didn't appear to be even vaguely canine. There were a couple of quite aggressive looking tortoises, for one thing.

The weirdness of those parts of the hunt paled in significance, however, next to the riders. Some of them were tall, elegant beings with pointed ears sticking out from under their riding helmets. Others were short, stocky, and bearded. A few were a sickly kind of greenish-grey, with slits for eyes, while others seemed to be hardly there at all, merely wispy outlines atop their steeds. Given the strangeness of all that, Eleanor felt more than justified in joining Norman in staring.

One of the lead riders, a woman of apparently unearthly beauty (though still not nearly enough to make jodhpurs work) looked down at the pair of them.

"What's going on? Are you two here to be prey, or what?"

Prey? Eleanor looked at Norman. Norman looked back at her, then reached out for her hand. He said what was possibly the only thing to be said, under the circumstances.

"Run!"

They ran. Eleanor had never been much of a runner, though it occurred to her as she sprinted away from the strange hunt behind them that she had become a little better at it since meeting Norman. Perhaps it had something to do with all the opportunities to practice. She ran through the trees, doing her best to keep up with Norman as he dodged and jinked, making it hard for the horses behind to follow.

They followed anyway, finding ways through the trees or at least following parallel to them. One of the horned horses—call it what it was: a unicorn—leapt a fallen tree, and its rider blew a small bugle as they landed. Behind that rider, the rest of the hunt kept pace.

That was the strange thing. They kept pace, but they didn't catch up. Eleanor had expected to be run down by the hunt in a matter of seconds, even with the cover of the trees to help them. yet they were somehow managing to keep ahead of it. However, to be fair, given that they were currently being chased by a collection of apparently mythical creatures, it was quite a long way down any potential list of strange things Eleanor could come up with.

Another slightly strange thing came in the form of the trees. There seemed to be a lot more of them than there had appeared to be when Eleanor had been laying in a ditch earlier. Then, it had seemed like there were only just enough to qualify as a small copse, yet now, she was sure that she had been running through them for more than a couple of minutes without stopping. Talking of which…

"Norman, I don't think I can keep going."

"You have to, Eleanor, unless you want to be ripped apart."

"Surely if we just talked to them…"

"*Talk* to them? Do you think they're going to give us the chance? Besides, I am *not* talking to people like *that*. Now come on."

They ran on, leaping logs and pushing through shin deep patches of mud. Specifically, Eleanor ran on until she tripped over one of the former and landed face first in one of the latter. She stood up.

"Run, Eleanor!" Norman insisted.

Eleanor shook her head. “I’ve had enough.”

“You’ve had enough? Do you think that’s going to be something they care about? People on horseback never care about the plight of the little person—particularly not when said little person has just tried to sabotage their hunt.”

“Yes, but *I* didn’t-”

“Really, so you weren’t here for the cause?”

“No, you idiot, I was here because you were. And frankly, I’m starting to think that was a mistake. Now, I’m going to talk to them.”

“No!” Norman’s hand clamped onto her arm. “That would be a betrayal of the cause—a betrayal of everything we believe in! There can’t be any talking with people who think the kinds of things they think! There can only be action!”

“What? The action of running away?”

“In this case.”

The good thing about being covered in mud was that it made it really quite easy for Eleanor to pull free of Norman’s grip. It didn’t quite make up for all the bad things about being covered in mud, but it was a start. Eleanor looked back to where the hunt was advancing on them. So did Norman.

“Eleanor, please.”

“It’s time we just talked this through like reasonable, rational human beings, Norman.”

Norman shook his head. “I should have known that your heart wasn’t in it,” he said before running off once more.

Part of the hunt ran past Eleanor to head after him. A couple more of the large dogs stopped at her, sniffing and yapping as a few of the horses came to a halt.

"What are you doing?" the woman who had been leading the hunt, when it started chasing them, demanded. "You've hardly run at all so far. Honestly, if you think we're paying you for such a limited display of running away then-"

"Look," Eleanor said, "I don't know what's going on, but you have no right to chase me and my… me and Norman or tiny people in red hats. So just stop, all right."

"Stop? After we've paid the little blighter perfectly good faerie gold to let us chase him? And you, of course, although I didn't realize there was going to be a relay element to it all."

"Relay element?" Eleanor tried her best to wipe some of the mud from her face. "What are you talking about?"

"Well, obviously…" The very beautiful woman in the jodhpurs looked momentarily confused. "Hold on, you were running from us because you were hired to do so by a gnome in a bar, weren't you?"

"No. I was running from you because I was being chased by all that." Eleanor made a gesture that happened to take in the giant hounds and the flame breathing horses. It was quite hard for it not to, really. "Oh, and because Norman said that what you were doing was monstrously cruel, and that we should sabotage it to stop it."

"Cruel?" The woman looked aghast. "What's cruel about chasing a few gnomes? It's not like they're foxes or anything."

“Um…” this conversation was rapidly getting out of Eleanor’s depth. “I’m fairly sure it must be worse, somehow.”

“Look,” the other woman said. “I’m Nivea.”

“Eleanor.”

“Well, Eleanor, it looks like this hunt’s done for, or it will be when your friend stops running… So, why don’t we head back to my place? It’s not far; you can get cleaned up; and then you can explain to me what’s so cruel about chasing gnomes, all right?”

Norman would have rejected the offer out of hand, of course. He would have called it consorting with the enemy. Eleanor didn’t care quite so much, at least if the consorting in question happened to include a shower somewhere along the line.

“All right,” she said. “Thanks. Um… how far is not far? I think I may have twisted my ankle.”

“Oh,” Nivea replied, snapping her fingers in a way that made a tower of white stone appear a few feet away, “not far at all.”

After Eleanor had taken a shower and borrowed some of Nivea’s old clothes, they took tea in a drawing room so far off the ground Eleanor was surprised it wasn’t a danger to low flying aircraft.

“Now,” Nivea said, “would you like to explain to me what’s so cruel about chasing a few gnomes?”

“Well,” Eleanor tried. “You’re chasing them.”

“Yes, absolutely. And?”

“Well, probably you shouldn’t be going around chasing things, and scaring them, and ripping them to pieces with large dogs.”

"Really? But it's what we pay them for. Well, except for the whole ripping them to pieces thing. I'm not sure anyone does that."

It took a while for those words to sink in—one small subset of them in particular. "You pay them? And you don't do anything to them? You mean this is like some sort of drag hunting?"

"Oh, no," Nivea said. "They're an endangered species; they don't run very fast; they tend to set fire to nearby trees; and if they knock a tooth out, you're suddenly facing an army of unstoppable skeletal warriors."

"Drag, not dragon—as in someone laying a trail for you to follow."

"That's the one," Nivea said with a nod. "Although mostly, we just follow the little red hats. It can cause trouble if we run into unexpected fire-fighters, but it's mostly just good clean fun."

That hadn't been what Norman had told her was happening. But then, knowing Norman, he wouldn't have stopped to check things thoroughly. He would have been too busy feeling righteously angry to bother. It occurred to Eleanor that she hadn't exactly checked things either; she'd just gone along with Norman.

"And no one gets hurt?" Eleanor asked.

"Well, one of the kelpies did drag its rider into a stream once, but if you mean with the dogs… gosh, no. We don't go in for that sort of thing. They just like to chase ever so slightly behind things. In fact, as long as someone runs, my dogs will keep chasing. You don't want to see what they get like when I'm working out on a treadmill."

Eleanor tried not to picture that one. She was too busy looking out through one of the windows of the tower. Down below, *far* down below, she thought that she could just about make out a human-sized figure running through the trees.

"Oh, that's right," Nivea said, moving up alongside Eleanor. "Some of the hunt is still chasing that friend of yours. I'd best go down and call them off."

Eleanor reached out to put a hand on the faerie woman's arm. "There's no rush. Norman can stop them at any time by just talking to them like I did, right?"

"Well… yes, but it doesn't seem like he's about to, does it?"

Eleanor smiled, and for a moment, she found herself thinking of every protest she'd been dragged along to where Norman had been right in the front line and where that had meant Eleanor had been right there next to him when the trouble started.

"No," she said happily, "I don't think that he is."

A Life of Conquest

It isn't easy being conquered, you know. Oh, I don't mean just the fighting and the killing and the rest of it. Frankly, on Pacifica, we've become quite used to that sort of thing over the years, what with being perched in the middle of the Forbidden Sector, where half a dozen planetary empires seem to feel the need to vie for supremacy. That's normal, and we've generally found that a policy of rapid surrender to any approaching force does the trick quite nicely.

And as a barman, things can potentially even go quite well. After all, one of the things any approaching horde invariably wants is a nice drink at the end of it, right? They even tend to pay for it, so long as I manage to work out which ones are the officers in time to give them free drinks and establish whether they happen to be allergic to bourbon. I'll tell you, I'm not making that mistake again after what happened when we were invaded by the lobster folk of Boilit Two, even if it did mean that invasion was a bit shorter than usual.

It's just that, recently, things have gotten a bit more complicated. Ordinarily, Pacifica's completely indefensible nature and lack of meaningful strategic importance mean that people tend to give it up fairly quickly, which is obviously fine by us. A high turnover of intergalactic oppressors keeps the economy moving, and all that, even if it often spends its time moving into said oppressors' pockets.

Maybe things would have gone a little better if someone had mentioned that idea to the Warmongers of Battle Planet One—not for the person doing the telling, obviously. They would have had a few problems in line with the ancient Warmonger principle of "Don't shoot the messenger, not when you can disembowel the messenger and then use his or her head as a handy drinking utensil." Still, it would have saved the rest of us a bit of bother when the Machines of Zappit Six showed up. There's nothing like finding somewhere double booked to take the fun out of a galactic conquest.

It wouldn't have been so bad if they had just fought a big battle to determine who owned the planet and got it over with. But, no, they had to go around trying to be dignified about it, which means that currently they're trying to ignore one another, hoping that eventually the other lot will go away, leaving them as sole masters of the planet.

That is not a very considerate plan, from where I'm standing. It means that one minute, you've got dreadlocked brutes wandering down the street beheading anyone who looks at them funnily, which is to say not in the infra-red spectrum; and the next, you have machines rolling along telling people that anything less than perfect order will result in their extermination. How exactly is someone meant to be orderly while trying to run along with his head hunched in so that his neck doesn't present too tempting a target for a battle blade? And when they're both on the same street, studiously ignoring one another, well, where exactly can you stand without appearing to support the wrong lot?

Then there are the laws they expect us to follow. Don't get me wrong, we here on Pacifica are pretty flexible when it comes to tyrannical dictates. Over the years, we've put up with everything from curfews to taxes, conscription to laws about what kind of hat we can wear. But you tell me, how exactly are we meant to conform to both an essentially tribal system based on resolving disputes through an ancient process based on extreme violence, *and* a strict interpretation of Asimov's Laws of Computing? And how, if those laws are so important, could the machines invade in the first place? Hypocrisy, that's what I call it.

Sorry, I got a bit carried away there. I wouldn't want to offend anyone—particularly not anyone with access to automated targeting systems. It's just… well, it hasn't been easy in the bar trade recently. One lot demands high grade motor oil by the gallon, while the other is drinking either the blood of their slain foes or milk. Where am I supposed to get milk? That's what I want to know. I'm a barman, not a dairy farmer.

And of course, now they've all gone and chosen my bar as their favorite one. It's very flattering, obviously. If they're drinking here, it at least means that they aren't drinking down at the Flamingo Club down the street, like invaders usually do, but I can't help feeling that it's putting me in an awkward position. Eventually, having everyone crammed into one room is going to mean a fight, even though I've done my best to keep the machines and the warmongers separated. You know, holding the machines' Kraftwerk karaoke and the

Warmongers' unhappy hour as far apart as possible—that kind of thing.

And it means that one of the resistance groups that always spring up is accusing me of being a collaborator. I've tried telling them that of course I am, and so is almost everyone on the planet. I've tried telling them that's how Pacifica *works,* but do they listen? Of course not. Frankly, the only way I've been able to keep them from shooting me as some kind of example is by offering to let them use the bar as a headquarters. You can say what you like about murderous oppressors, but at least they don't expect to be allowed to use the pool table for free.

So sooner or later, the odds are that my bar is going to be blown up by one side or another, which is a nuisance any way you look at it—even with the insurance. I mean, do you know what premiums are like on a planet that is subjected to a full bombardment every three years on average? Leave? What are you talking about? This is my home. I haven't spent a lifetime surrendering to anyone who comes along just to give in, have I?

No, I've got a better plan than that anyway. I spent an hour last week getting a bunch of leaflets printed up extolling the virtues of the machine and warmonger planets, after a couple of earlier hours spent *finding* some virtues. It wasn't that hard. I just based them on the usual ones our tourist board puts out—you know, the ones with "Why Not Conquer Pacifica This Summer?" and all that. You must have seen them.

Really, it was just a question of packaging together the stuff *their* tourist boards put out, although I must say I'm not sure about the slogan "resistance is futile" for the machines. I'm fairly sure that's *our* planetary motto, for one thing—not that I'm complaining if they want to use it, of course. Perish the thought, or possibly just perish, if I complain too loudly.

Now I'm sure you can see what I've been doing, can't you? Oh, you can't? Leaving them out so that they'll get homesick and head back? It's a nice idea, but I generally find that when someone sets out to conquer the known universe, it's because home isn't exactly the kind of place to get homesick at the thought of. Sick, possibly, but not homesick.

No, it's far easier just to leave them out when the other lot are drinking—nice little leaflets, mentioning the cultural high points of the planet, like the traditional combat to the death and poetry festival the warmongers have. Oh, and also just happening to mention that, since the other side is busy trying to conquer Pacifica, there isn't anyone home to man (or machine) the defenses at the moment.

I reckon they'll probably be gone by Tuesday, after which I'll probably get a medal from the resistance, assuming that the leaflets pointing out the existence of even more oppressed planets across the sector haven't done the trick by that point. Now, excuse me, I've got a tanker full of machine oil in the back and not a lot of time left in which to shift it.

The Middle of Nowhere

"We're lost, aren't we?" Sandra asked, looking around at the place she and Mike currently found themselves in. There wasn't a great deal to look at, unless you liked rolling hills covered in scrub, cactus, and the odd sheep. Sandra didn't.

"Why do you think we're lost?" Mike retorted.

"Because we're in the middle of nowhere, you keep looking at the map like you don't know which way up is meant to be, and anyway, I think we passed that sheep an hour ago. We're going in circles."

Mike stopped and adjusted his hat. Sandra had acquired a particular loathing for that hat over the past few days. That and the bullwhip he insisted on carrying around. What did he think he was going to do with it? The one time Sandra had seen Mike practicing with it, he had nearly taken his own head off. It wasn't any way for an archaeology professor to behave.

But then, he didn't behave that way even when he was nominally doing archaeology. When Sandra had been learning the subject as part of her wider interest in anthropology, before she signed on as Dr. M. Cincinnati's grad student, she had been told that it involved careful analysis, the consistent use of recording techniques, and some solid abilities with a trowel. There had been no mention of (just to pick an example or two at random) running away from giant boulders, being shot at by indigenous peoples with an array of authentic tribal weaponry, or hanging perilously above sudden drops. It was, Sandra felt, something they hadn't mentioned for a reason.

"Are you sure we're lost?" Mike asked.

Sandra sighed. "To be honest, I suspect that you've been holding the map the wrong way up for at least the last hour."

"Great!" Mike actually punched the air; although given how well he did in the barroom brawls they always seemed to get into in small towns Sandra hadn't heard of, he probably missed.

"Great?" Sandra looked down at her sand covered clothes, considered how far they probably were from a hot shower, and sighed. "How can that possibly be great?"

"Well, we're looking for the lost city of Um, right?"

"Right." Apparently—although Sandra didn't particularly remember asking to go on an adventure across three continents in an effort to bolster Mike Harding's reputation as an archaeological adventurer. She'd just wanted something for her final thesis. Right now, she was considering whether a study of delusions in academic personnel would get her very far.

"A city so thoroughly lost that all people can say when you ask for directions is 'um…'? A city that has never been so much as glimpsed by foreign eyes, and which will undoubtedly show all those people who have mocked me that I was right all along."

"Right about what?" Sandra asked.

Mike hesitated. "You know, just generally right."

"What does all this have to do with you holding the map the wrong way up," Sandra demanded.

Mike gestured to the map. "Well, the way I see it, if you want to find somewhere that has been lost, first you have to get pretty thoroughly lost yourself. I figured that if we were to get so spectacularly lost that you could only achieve greater confusion by using a Sat Nav system, then logically, we should be exactly where Um is. Why, I wouldn't be surprised if the whole place were just over that next rise."

Mike actually set out towards the rise in question, striding the confident strides of someone who spent an hour every morning practicing his heroic striding. While he got on with that, Sandra turned her finely tuned academic brain to the logic of the idea he had just put forward—which mostly meant that she had to run to catch up once she came to a conclusion. She caught up with her supervisor just a few strides from the top.

"Mike, you do realize that your whole approach is the biggest load of rubbish I've heard since the notion of a uniform Celtic monoculture in pre-Roman Europe?"

"You think so?" Mike asked, reaching the top.

"Of *course* I think so," Sandra shot back.

Mike swept out an arm. "Then what's that?"

Sandra followed the sweep of the limb with her eyes. Below, spread along the bottom of a valley, made from ancient looking stone and with occasional monuments sticking up between them, were houses.

"That," Sandra said, "is a complete coincidence, and it does nothing to invalidate my argument."

Mike grinned. "Let's go down and have a look, shall we?"

It was undoubtedly Um. The sign at the edge of town said so—well, not so much a sign as a rock with the word UM carved into it in big letters. *A lost city that knew what people called it,* Sandra thought. *Interesting.* And also logically impossible, when you thought about the definition of the word "lost".

Mike, of course, was thinking of other things.

"There will almost certainly be traps and pitfalls," he said, "so watch your step, or at least try to fall in a way that lets me grab your wrist at the last moment and pull you up."

Sandra very carefully didn't point out that most of the time it was her pulling Mike out of the pits, and that he could do with losing a few pounds if he planned on being pulled up on a regular basis.

"Oh, and watch out for snake priests worshiping long dead things with unpronounceable names. If you aren't careful in these lost cities, you can end up sacrificed by pitiless locals before you've had chance to say, 'Can I interview you for my research project?' which is always a nuisance."

That was one way of putting it, certainly—although Sandra suspected that the odds of there being anyone actually alive in a place like this was… oh. They came out of the little stone houses in ones and twos, covered in dark cloaks and shuffling forward.

"What did I say?" Mike said. "Snake priests. Now, where did I put my whip?"

Sandra sighed and looked back to the approaching figures. "Hi, there."

"Hello," one of the lead figures said, removing the cloak that protected it against the wilderness elements. Beneath was a perfectly pleasant looking woman in her fifties. "Welcome to Um. Are you lost? No, that's a silly question, isn't it? You're in Um. You must be lost."

"Actually," Mike said. "We have found what we were looking for. We have been searching for Um for a long time, and now here it is. I'm an archaeologist, incidentally."

"Really?" the woman said. "What a coincidence. So am I."

The woman, whose name turned out to be Rose, invited them into her ancient stone complex for tea.

"Please don't mind the mess. One of the minor joys of having so few visitors, you see."

The tea was good, and it was drunk out of a prehistoric stone beaker in Sandra's case. Rose had a mug with 'to the world's greatest grandma' on it, while Mike got a plastic cup. He looked a bit dejected, which wasn't exactly the expression Sandra had expected so soon after successfully concluding his search for the city. Frankly though, she was too busy talking to Rose to bother too much.

"So you found this place twenty years ago?" Sandra asked.

"That's right, dear. I expect people probably thought I was lost in the desert—which I was, obviously. You have to get very lost to find

Um. I got here, and I looked around, and it seemed like such a lovely place that I decided to settle down."

"Just like that?" Sandra asked. "What about everybody left behind?"

"Oh, there weren't many people. You probably know how it is dear, running after your academic career, not much time to get out and have a life."

Sandra resented that. She had a life. She had friends. Admittedly, she hadn't seen the majority of them face to face in more than a year, what with trying to keep up with Mike, but that wasn't the point. She had a life. Or at least, she could have one if she ever wanted to. Probably.

"Well, what *about* your career then?" Sandra asked. "Presumably, you gave up a lot by staying here?"

"Oh, not as much as I thought at the time. I don't have a host of academic papers to my name, but then I'm not fighting every day trying to advance my career either. I'm not caught up in endless departmental meetings. And I never, *never* have to go to conferences. But then, that's mostly what Um is about."

Sandra looked over to Mike who shook his head. Apparently, he didn't understand either.

"I'm sorry," she said, "you've lost us."

Rose laughed gently. "Well, yes, this is Um." She smiled at Mike. "From the looks of you, I imagine you want to go and have a look around, so why don't you do that while I have a talk to Sandra here?"

Mike shot away so fast Sandra thought he might have been fired from a cannon, which had actually happened once, in Guatemala.

"Now, I suppose I should start by explaining the history of this place," Rose said once Mike was gone.

"It certainly looks old," Sandra said. "How old? A thousand years? Two? Four?"

"Something like that." Rose shrugged as she said it. "When Um was discovered back in the eighteenth century, there were inscriptions there in a mixture of Ancient Greek and Egyptian, I understand."

"Um was discovered way back then?" Sandra asked. That didn't seem to make sense. "If that's true, why didn't we hear about it? I mean, the only expedition I know about in the area is the one of Sir Joshua Weatherby in 1795, and that-"

"That's the one," Rose said, putting her tea down. "He got utterly tired of his job in the emerging civil service and set out to discover things. He set off into the desert without even the endless train of hangers one normally required of the gentleman adventurer. And he found Um. Since then, of course, it has been discovered by a great many other people." Rose smiled. "Including you and your friend."

Sandra shook her head. "But that can't be right, can it? I mean, places can only be discovered once." She thought for a moment. "Places other than America can only be discovered once. And Weatherby didn't discover anywhere. He disappeared."

Rose shook her head and extended a hand. "He stayed. Come on. While your friend is busy photographing inscriptions, I'll show you round properly."

Sandra thought for a moment, and then she let the other woman help her to her feet. After all, she was meant to be here to learn things, wasn't she?

Sandra followed Rose around the city, watching people go past as Rose pointed out the architecture, the inscriptions, the stonework, and all the other things that Sandra guessed that she should have been interested in as an archaeologist. She was actually more interested in the people. With their hoods down, Sandra could see that there were people there from all kinds of places and times of life. They were mostly quietly pleasant to one another and to Sandra, nodding as she and Rose passed or saying hello. They didn't look to be in any kind of hurry.

"Who are these people?" Sandra asked.

"Oh, they're mostly just people who have gotten lost, like me," Rose said. "A few of them are the children of people who have gotten lost, but they mostly go out into the world to be found again for a while. Nobody minds."

"You make it sound like people are choosing whether to be lost or not," Sandra said.

Rose smiled. "How else do you think they got this lost? These days, what with satellite mapping and GPS, people could find themselves pretty easily if they wanted to. Even when I first came here, the only way you could get really, properly lost was if you made an effort."

Sandra tried to wrap her head around that. "People are getting lost *deliberately*?"

The other woman smiled again. "We get all sorts here. Burnt out businessmen. People who just want to start again. Accountants. We have quite a lot of accountants, but it's a good place for all that."

Sandra shook her head. "It doesn't make any sense."

"Doesn't it?" Rose looked at her carefully. "You found this place, after all. I don't think it was your friend who managed it. Why don't you sit and have a think about it? Some of the old stones are quite comfy, I find."

Sandra sat down on what looked like a several thousand-year-old memorial. It was indeed more comfortable than it looked.

"But how does this place run?" she asked. "I mean, you must get things from outside."

"Oh, the internet is a useful thing, and we get a few web types, so that's easy enough."

"But money-"

"We're in a city full of ancient treasures, and quite a few of our incomers have money. Even Weatherby left plenty."

It sounded so easy, but Sandra knew that nothing was that easy. Life was about working hard and getting to where you deserved to be. She had, after all, put up with Mike Harding just so that she could get the kind of academic career she knew she ought to have.

“I can see you have a lot to think about,” Rose said, standing up, but Sandra wasn’t listening.

Sandra found Mike in the middle of an ancient temple, taking pictures with his camera phone of mosaics, while standing amid a collection of stone jars that looked like they had been made back when asses’ milk was the bathing material of choice—actually, to be more specific, the remains of a couple of jars, given that Mike wasn’t exactly the most careful of men when he was busy photographing ancient art.

Sandra walked in and coughed to get his attention. Mike turned, and another jar went crashing to the ground.

“Now look what you made me do.”

“Right,” Sandra said. “Sorry.”

“Did you get plenty of information on this place out of that woman?”

“Rose.”

“Whatever. It’s important to have plenty of information when you’re discovering places. Plus, you’ll need enough to use as data for your thesis, of course.”

Ah, yes, her thesis—ninety thousand words to write, all about this place—presumably immediately making it the center of a whole research cottage industry.

“I can see it now,” Mike said. “You’ll have your PhD, and I’ll have my research funding for the next ten years, plus probably a professorship. Actually, forget that. I’ll get my own department out of this. Plus, there will be papers, and books, and appearances at conferences to-"

"Mike."

"Of course, you'd have full joint authorship. With my name first, of course, since I'm the senior academic here, and probably with you as et al in the abbreviated editions, but definitely in there somewhere."

"Mike?"

"Hmm... I hope that Rose isn't going to try to claim that *she* discovered Um. That wouldn't be helpful at all. I mean, we'd have to find some way to discredit her findings, or prove that they weren't properly documented, or... well it would make things awkward at the conferences, and you know what things get like at the conferences."

Sandra knew. It was the conferences, ultimately, that had helped her to decide.

"*Mike.*"

"Yes?"

"I'm not sure if I want to go back."

"What? Don't be stupid, Sandra. Of course you want to go back. There's so much there for you now—so much there for both of us."

And that was the problem, of course. "So much" in this context just meant more work. It meant spending time in rooms with people she didn't much like—people not entirely unlike Mike Harding. It meant finishing all the endless research for her thesis, of course, but *that* just meant starting more research. All on a place that emphatically didn't want to be researched.

"Mike, I think we should leave this," she said. "I think you should just go home and forget about Um."

"Forget about it? Now you really are being stupid. Has the heat gotten to you or something? We could get whole *careers* out of this."

Sandra could see from Mike's expression that she wasn't going to change his mind. "You're right," she said, "but you're going to need more pictures of that mosaic to convince people."

Mike nodded and turned back to it. Sandra very carefully picked up one of the jars. It seemed a waste, but not nearly as much of one as it would have seemed an hour or two ago. As she lifted it, it occurred to her that she was going to have to delete Mike's notes and pictures, then drive him back to civilization before he got over the concussion, and then probably spend some time persuading people that he'd been out in the heat too long, because she certainly hadn't seen anything. It was a lot of work just to get well and truly lost.

But it was, she decided, as she brought the jar down, almost certainly going to be worth it.

It's Only A...

Antonia431 was at home, accumulating what she hoped was going to be her highest daily score for a Saturday ever in the Game. First, she did some washing. Then, she tidied the house a little. She sat down and read for a while, because everyone knew that the algorithms of the Game liked people to vary what they did, and then she went out shopping. All the while, the automated score counter on her wrist spun, racking up the points for every interaction. She had a date planned for later that night, which would hopefully push the thing round even further, at least assuming things went well.

The Game was such a simple idea. It was realer than real life, at least according to the marketing people, especially after everything that had happened with the Great Disaster. And it was *fun,* even if the reality of the programming, coupled with the integrated feedback sensors, occasionally made it feel otherwise. Even on those occasions though, Antonia could feel happy that she was still racking up points towards her score.

Talking of which, Antonia decided to take the trash out. After all, she'd noticed a distinct correlation between doing it and extra points, even if it didn't happen all the time. As people had pointed out, the Game's unpredictability was part of what made it so great. So she got the trash and went out into the yard with it, confident that it would add at least another point or two to her total.

She was slightly less confident when someone hit her over the head with something, however, even if it did suggest that she'd uncovered a bonus level.

Antonia431 hadn't been tied to a chair in an apparently abandoned warehouse many times before. Despite that comparative lack of experience, however, she felt that she was still well placed to make the one obvious observation about it. It sucked. Honestly, if this was the best that virtual reality had to offer, then they needed to get some better scriptwriters in.

"Hey! Is there anyone there?"

No one answered immediately. Maybe that meant that she was supposed to deal with this alone, like some kind of puzzle game. Antonia didn't particularly like those, partly because she preferred just the main Game to any of the sub-games that had sprung up within it, and partly because they meant getting into the heads of the people who had designed them. That was kind of hard, given how odd some of those heads seemed to be sometimes. Here, for example, there seemed to be no handy tools, just a quick roll away, while the knots were impossible for her to get her fingers to. It was at times like this she found herself thinking about those people who claimed to have been able to hack the system. The ability to extend her fingers beyond the normal limits of the program would have made things a lot easier.

No, Antonia reminded herself, that was cheating. That wasn't fun. Of course, nor was sitting in a chair right then, but that was presumably just the result of the automatically adaptive difficulty settings. Obviously, she'd had things a bit too easy in the Game recently. So she did her best, trying to come up with alternate solutions. Unfortunately, the only one that sprang to mind involved dislocating her own elbows, and thanks to the Game's integrated feedback system, that would hurt. It might even cost her life points.

Besides, it turned out that she didn't have time. Even as Antonia watched, three figures approached from the darkness of the warehouse—two men and a woman. All wore long black leather coats, as well as sunglasses. How they didn't bump into things in the dark wasn't readily apparent.

"Who are you?" Antonia demanded. "What do you want? Come on, you have to tell me your usernames. It's in the rulebook."

"We don't care about the rulebook," one of the men said. His avatar was quite short and fat, which was quite unusual. Most people played the training sub-games until their avatars looked more like the norm.

"We have no usernames," the other man said. He was tall, skinny, and had an assortment of pens sticking out of the pocket of his leather coat. "Where there is no user, how can there be a name?"

"Also, what is the sound of one hand clapping?" the first man added.

The woman with them sighed and removed her sunglasses. She was quite pretty in a couldn't care less way, with hacked short dark hair and an almost total absence of the multiple piercings and tattoos most people used to decorate their avatars.

"Guys," she said, "what have I told you about being all mysterious and pseudo-philosophical at people?"

"Um..." the skinnier of the two men began, "that you'd kick us both really hard if we... *ouch*!"

"Exactly. Also, who told you to tie her up?"

"Well, we had to fetch you, didn't we?" the first one complained. "We couldn't just- ow, sorry, Brenda."

Brenda? What kind of a username was Brenda? Maybe it was just a shortened form, the way Antonia431 tended to drop the number in her head.

"You must be very confused, Antonia," Brenda said as she undid the ropes. "I imagine you can't tell what genre you're in at all."

"I thought it might be puzzle," Antonia said. "Maybe it's just a very weird RPG though."

Brenda nodded, "I can see why you might say it, but no."

"Platformer? Beat 'em up?"

"Do Adam and Mitchell look like they'd do well in beat 'em up territory?" Brenda asked.

"Comedy beat 'em up then," Antonia tried. "Or maybe some kind of sci-fi adventure thing."

Brenda shook her head. "Sorry, no. The truth is, Antonia, that you aren't in a game at all."

"Of course I am," Antonia snapped back, starting to stand. "This is the Game, isn't it? Now, I don't know what kind of useless Easter Egg this is meant to be, but-"

Brenda sighed. “Antonia, I’m going to tell you something important now, and I want you to hear me out, okay. There. Is. No. Game. This… I’m sorry to say this, Antonia, but this is the real world.”

Antonia sat there while Brenda started to explain. She explained that the population of Earth was not held in highly enjoyable VR pods following the Great Disaster, and that there hadn’t been the combination of floods, earthquakes, radiation leaks, and coffee shortages everyone tended to assume.

“Well, what was it then?” Antonia demanded. Usually, if you were impatient enough, you could get through cut sequences like this pretty quickly.

Brenda shrugged. “Apathy. The Great Disaster was nobody being bothered anymore. It was nobody going to work, nobody bothering to vote, nobody *caring*... Mostly, they were all too busy playing video games.”

“So how does putting everyone in VR solve that?” Antonia demanded. “You really have to think these things through, you know, before you come out with dialogue like that.”

“It’s not dialogue,” Brenda said. “I’m just talking to you. There’s a difference… and I never said anyone was put in VR. Just the opposite, in fact.”

Clearly, this scene wasn’t going to be skippable even if Antonia was rude. How annoying. Oh, well, as people always said, best to play along. It’s only the Game, after all.

“What’s the opposite of VR?” Antonia demanded.

Brenda gestured to the world around her. "They came up with the Game."

"So they *did-*"

"The Game is an elaborate fiction," Brenda went on. "One morning, about a century or so ago, the governments agreed to do the same thing. They started to *tell* people that they had put them into a virtual reality game. It took a bit of doing, because people thought that they could remember whole lives, but they got around that by having a few carefully planted stooges 'remember' being put into the machines.

"After that… well, it caught on pretty comprehensively, all things considered. And when people refused to comply, there was always the option of designating them an enemy in a shooter. They don't do that so much these days, but only because people volunteer. A genuine multiplayer experience, they call it."

"That's…" Antonia struggled for the words to express just how insane she thought Brenda and her cronies were. "You've got a bad patch of code, or something. This is the Game. It's a game. That's why they *call* it the Game."

"Really?" Brenda asked. "If this is a computer game, full of extra lives, and all the possibilities that go with being in VR, why are most people's lives so humdrum?"

"You just said yourself: there are shooters and beat 'em ups and…"

"Before the Game, they called those things 'going paintballing' and 'getting beaten up'. Besides, you know what I mean. Those things aren't everywhere. Those things are just a tenth of one percent of people's lives, if that. Most people's lives are *boring*." Brenda looked around her. "Take this place, for example. You were tied up here for almost an hour, with nothing happening. Does that sound like good scene management to you?"

Antonia wasn't going to let them get to her. "That happens a lot. Who knows what points we're racking up at bus stops and in post office queues? In fact, if this isn't a game, why are we getting points at all?" She held up her wrist triumphantly, though it might have been better if her point counter had still been there.

Adam held out something to Brenda, who took it from him. It was Antonia's counter. Very carefully, Brenda put it on the floor.

"Look at it," she demanded.

Antonia looked. "I don't get what you want me to see. It's a perfectly ordinary counter, with the numbers going round just as they should."

"Just as they should?" Brenda countered. "You aren't doing anything. How can you be accumulating points if you aren't doing anything?"

"Well-"

"And it isn't even on your body. It isn't connected to you, so it can't be counting your points. Yet it's still going up."

That was, Antonia had to admit, a bit odd—almost as odd as the feeling of it not being on her wrist. No one took their counters off. The rumor was that it could cause all kinds of glitches. Actually, maybe that was what this was: some giant, elaborate, glitch caused by the removal of her point counter.

"We need to take extreme measures," Brenda said to the other two. "She still isn't getting it. Bring in the box."

Well, that sounded ominous. It even looked ominous when the two men with Brenda came back with a box featuring a number of wires coming out of it, along with a screen.

"Look," Antonia said, "I'm sure we can all get through this without having to-"

Adam turned on the device, and passed her a smaller box with a number of buttons and switches sticking out. On the screen, people appeared. Tentatively, Antonia pressed a button. One of the people crouched down, then stood up again when she pressed it once more.

"It's a video game," Brenda explained. "This is what they're really like. Go on, try it."

Antonia did, and she had to admit, she quite enjoyed it. At least until she realized the obvious point. "My life is nothing like this. I hardly ever get eaten by carnivorous plants coming out of pipes, for one thing."

"That's because your life is real," Brenda insisted. She trod on Antonia's points counter very deliberately. "Those things are designed to change at random. People spend their lives trying to work out what they should be doing to get points, but the truth is, it doesn't make any difference. You're just living your life."

That hit Antonia like a lead weight. "But if that's true, then none of it means anything. There are no high scores, no leader boards…"

Brenda shook her head. "It means plenty. It just isn't a game. It's *more* than a game."

Right then, Antonia wasn't sure that she could see it. She could just see the massive injustice of the system around her. What was the point of it? Convincing people to engage with it? Well, she'd engage with it, all right.

"So, I take it the point of all this is to recruit me into a band of dedicated freedom fighters, determined to bring down the corruption of the system?" she asked. Ten minutes ago, she wouldn't have been willing to join such a thing, but that had been then.

Brenda's eyebrow's beetled together. "What do you mean?"

"All this. It's a lot of trouble to go to, so I assume that you must be trying to undo the damage caused by the Game, right?"

Brenda laughed. "Are you *kidding?* They'd kill us if we started doing that. What do you think we are, some kind of heroes?"

"Then why?" Antonia demanded.

"Well, we needed a fourth player for some of the multiplayer games on the old box, and we thought you might want to. Um… you *do* want to, right?"

Antonia hesitated. This was not exactly what she had been expecting. On the other hand, she had to admit it did sound better than being shot at by the government. And when you thought about it, what other way was there to resist in a world like this?

"All right," she said, "but I am *not* partnering up with Adam."

Enhanced

Miles Delaware sat at his desk, held his phone to his ear, and endeavored not to let the headache he was slowly developing get the better of him. With Norm Pettering, the team owner, on the other end of the line, it wasn't that simple—particularly when he was complaining once again about just how little the boys were winning this season.

It used to be fairly easy, being a football coach. Draw a few diagrams that none of the quarterbacks could understand anyway, shout at a few people, occasionally try to manage the midseason injury crisis before it got rid of the whole offensive line—easy. And if it all went wrong, you could always just say that you didn't have the talent to work with. It didn't make any difference when they were firing you, generally, but you could say it.

Now, though, things had changed.

"Things have changed, Miles," Norm told him.

"Are you reading my mind, Norm?"

"No, but you might want to consider that as one of your mutant picks."

"I've told you before, I'm not doing that kind of thing."

"You are if you want to keep running my team— or *any* team, these days. The world has moved on, Miles."

"But Norm-"

The owner hung up. The worst part, of course, was that Norm was right. The world *had* moved on—mostly thanks to scientists who didn't know much about football, but who did know quite a bit about giving things extra legs. Why they had to go around doing stuff like that, Miles didn't know.

No, that wasn't fair. There were plenty of medical applications for the new science of mutation inducement. Probably, an extra leg or two was very useful to a man without any. Miles could even see that some of the military applications had their place. It was just... sport? What place did tentacles and the knack of mind reading have in sport?

Quite a bit, it turned out, when a couple of years ago someone had pointed out that while every sport had rules about performance enhancing drugs, and that they were even enforced occasionally, no one had put in place rules banning mutations yet. After all, how would you phrase them? Besides, it turned out that people *liked* seeing athletes with kangaroo legs run the hundred meters in seven seconds. Who'd have thought it?

At first, no one much had done it, but then LA decided to lead the way with a couple of tentacled wide receivers. They'd won the Superbowl that season. Now... well, if your line didn't include at least one guy with super-strength and another with a turtle's shell, your guys were getting killed—literally, on occasions.

So the logical thing for Miles to do was just to turn around, get onto the mutagenic clinic, and order up a couple of linebackers with a train's worth of muscle mass and a lemming's instinct for self-preservation. Maybe he wouldn't even notice the difference. It was just… well, they *said* that they could undo that kind of thing at the end of a career, have a guy right back to normal, but Miles wasn't convinced. How did anyone remember what normal was after all that time? And what if they wouldn't *go* back to normal? What if they wanted to stick like that? What if…

No, no more what ifs. Miles knew what he had to do. He'd been told to do it by the owner, and the players wouldn't mind too much. They knew how it went. One guy did something, and if he got away with it, well… it became the price of getting to the top. That was just how it was. So, now, the only choice Miles had was really over whether he wanted naturally sticky hands for his receivers, one giant arm for the quarterback, or twelve-foot-tall running backs. For several seconds, he sat there, doodling on the pad he kept there just for that, trying to work out what combination offered the best bang for his buck. Players who could cover the ten yards in a single stride? Maybe. Or maybe he just needed better plans. After all, it was all about controlling things from the side-lines, wasn't it?

Miles picked up the phone and rang his boss. "Norm, how would you like to win a pennant or two?"

"What did you have in mind?"

In the stadium, the crowd roared as the two teams took the field. One looked comparatively normal, while the other had the now almost obligatory collection of extra parts. Miles didn't care. He just waited for the opposition to kick off, then he concentrated. The ball stopped in mid-air, darted down briefly to touch the foot of one of his players, and then shot back towards the opponent's goal like a bullet, passing between the uprights—the easiest field goal ever!

Beside Miles, Norm bit his fingernails. "I still don't know if this is allowed, Miles. I mean, you aren't on the field of play."

"Neither is any other coach, but they get to control the action pretty well. Now quiet, they're kicking again."

Another kick, another easy goal. This shouldn't take more than twenty or thirty more times.

"You realize that they'll try to shut you down?" Norm pointed out. "They *will* ban you from doing this from the side."

"Then I'll step out onto the field—just way away from the action."

"Well, then, they'll-"

Miles raised a brief hand for silence. Another field goal shot home. "What they'll do, Norm, is ban all use of mutations. It's the only thing they can really do. That, or they'll create an opening for an all-clean league, because after a game or two, no one will want to watch *this*."

Norm shrugged as the ball went arching through the air again. "So?"

Miles shook his head. "So when they do that, whose team is the only one whose best players are all currently mutation free, Norm?"

Norm thought about that for a moment, then smiled in that way he had when he'd just spotted something that could be worth money. "Why, I do believe it's mine, Miles."

Miles grinned. “Exactly. Now be quiet. I’ve got another goal to kick.”

And with a Spring...

Abilius Hexton III woke up in his own bed, looked around, and found that he wasn't sharing it with a couple of strangers he'd never seen before, nor was there a horse's head, or even a note left mysteriously on the bedside table— although that was possibly just because there wasn't a bedside table, either.

How odd.

He got up, showered, and got dressed. In that time, nobody interrupted with an urgent phone call, or burst in, or even shot at him through the bedroom window so that he was forced to take cover behind the bed. He went back and made the bed, checking it carefully to see if there was any sign that he might have missed a body rolled carefully under it. There wasn't.

Abilius tried to think of another morning when nothing like that had happened, and in all his twenty-five years, the only one that sprang to mind was the time when everybody had been too busy sitting downstairs in silence, thanks to the death of his parents. He hoped it wasn't going to be anything like that.

He went downstairs, made breakfast, and looked through the mail, of which there didn't seem to be much. All the bills were expected, and all the rest of it seemed to be perfectly ordinary junk mail. Hmm… this was starting to get slightly worrying. So worrying, in fact, that Abilius went to telephone his friend Frank, who worked down at the university. He went to do it and succeeded, without his attempted call being interrupted at all by some mysterious stranger telephoning at precisely the same instant. That was enough that Abilius could barely get the first few words out when Frank picked up.

"Frank… hi, it's me. Um… this is probably going to sound strange, but have you noticed anything weird happening?"

"I can't say I have," Frank replied. "In fact, nothing weird has happened to me all morning."

"Nothing weird has been happening to me either," Abilius said. "It's… weird. I was kind of hoping that you were going to tell me that I was imagining it. Or at least that it turns out you're my long-lost brother, or something."

"Sorry," Frank said. "Nothing like that. Besides, I've got five long lost brothers already."

"I've got six. Look, you don't think that something is happening, do you?"

"I don't know," Frank admitted. "Why don't you come down to the university, and we'll look into it properly?"

So Abilius drove to the university. It was possibly the single most boring drive of his life. He checked under the hood for unexpected car bombs, and he found that his fan belt was merely slightly frayed and would probably need replacing soon. The traffic was quiet, with an almost worrying lack of sudden crashes or people dropping from buildings onto hoods. Even the usual people who wandered back and forth with panes of glass for no apparent reason seemed to be a little more careful than usual.

The result was that Abilius got to Frank's department a good twenty minutes earlier than he had anticipated. Frank wasn't there yet, leaving Abilius sitting outside his office. Because he knew how these things worked, Abilius tried the handle of the office, fully expecting it to be unlocked and for Frank's body to be inside, but it wasn't, so he went back to waiting.

He didn't have to wait long, since apparently Frank wasn't slowed down by the usual traffic either. When his friend arrived, he ushered Abilius through to the office without so much as pausing to keel over having been assassinated to keep him from telling what he knew. Apparently though, that was mostly because he didn't know anything. Beyond confirming that nothing strange had happened to him that day, he didn't have any immediate answers.

He did, however, begin a few tests with Abilius's help. They started by making discrete inquiries with everyone from the departmental receptionist to a couple of passing students. Most of them looked surprisingly relieved when they mentioned it, saying that yes, it had happened (or rather not happened) to them too, and that wasn't it strange, things not being strange anymore. One of the students reported that he'd been rushing with an essay, trying to get it in on time, and he hadn't been tripped up, or had it stolen from him, or had to break off to deal with the imminent collapse of his relationship even once.

That seemed to confirm that the effect was general. Now the question was one of what it was. Frank ran a series of elaborate and outlandish looking devices over Abilius; none of which registered anything. On closer inspection, it turned out that was because most of them weren't working. Only when Frank went and got an old-fashioned mass spectrometer out did they get any kind of results at all.

"Interesting," Frank said, "the results seem to indicate that most of the usual elements are present around us, but that things are perfectly normal."

Abilius raised an eyebrow. "Things are never perfectly normal around here."

Frank nodded. "True, and that is generally due to the presence of a strong narrative event field around each atom. Now, I don't think that is quite gone, because all the usual markers for it seem to be there, but I'm sure something must be suppressing it. That's the only way I can think of to explain this sudden outbreak of realism."

"All right," Abilius asked. "What could suppress a field like that?"

"Possibly a contrasting literary field could do it, although you have to understand, that is just conjecture."

No one came in with a crucial bit of proof at that point. For Abilius, it was all the proof he needed.

"How soon will it destroy the world?" he asked. It was a well-known fact that any sudden discovery in the scientific field had to have the possibility of doing so. No one quite knew why.

"That's the worrying thing," Frank said. "From here, it looks like it won't."

"It won't?"

Frank shook his head. “Although obviously, it will have some pretty severe consequences if it goes on. I mean, people who find themselves short of money won’t be able to rely on checks from long lost uncles showing up in the mail anymore, and anyone who falls off a building… well, they might actually hit the ground instead of snagging on a handy flagpole.”

Put like that, the implications seemed more than worrying enough to be going on with. Abilius looked at his friend. “Is there anything we can do to counteract it?”

Frank shrugged. “I guess in theory, if we collect together a large enough pile of cheap thrillers, they should give off a pulse of narrative events large enough to collapse the field. Are you sure you want to do it though?”

“You just said how bad this could be,” Abilius pointed out.

“Yes, but it might not be like that. I mean, there are up sides too.”

Abilius raised an eyebrow. “Such as?”

“You haven’t been shot at today, nor have I. I haven’t had ex-wives I didn’t know about showing up unexpectedly. Neither of us has been suddenly diagnosed with anything incurable. Neither of us…”

“I understand,” Abilius said. “So you’re saying we shouldn’t do anything?”

Frank shrugged. “I’m not sure. I’ll tell you what; I’ll set it up, and while I do, why don’t you work on that side of things?”

“So you’re putting the whole decision on my shoulders?”

“Better you than me.”

Abilius took the hint and left Frank's office, wandering around the campus with no particular destination in mind. He was too busy thinking. Should they undo this, whatever it was? What would life be like without the twists and turns he'd come to expect? He sat down on a bench, first checking it for the inevitable secret message or parcel taped to the bottom. There was one, as it happened, but it looked to be a couple of days old, so Abilius put it in the nearest trash can. You couldn't have secret parcels cluttering up the place.

Of course, if they just left things, then presumably there wouldn't be very many of them soon. They would fade away from people's days along with car chases on the way to work, momentous announcements by colleagues at lunch, and the boss saying that because of some quirk of the company's finances, everyone was being relocated to Alaska. Abilius hated it when that happened.

So on that basis, he should probably rush back to tell Frank not to bother. After all, so many of the twists going around made life more difficult for people. All those long-lost relatives, for example, quickly added up come Thanksgiving. Then there were all the people shot, or blown up, or simply disappearing to think about. Presumably, that kind of thing wasn't much fun, and Abilius was in a position to declare a permanent end to it right now.

It was just… well, he looked out over the campus, and he saw students going about their normal days with the faintly bored looks of people whose attempts to revise for exams weren't being interrupted by the need to take life affirming road trips. He saw one of the prettier girls there breaking up with a geek rather than declaring her undying love for him. He even sat there for five whole minutes during which nothing much happened at all. Did anyone really want to live their lives like that?

Almost an hour later, Abilius went back to Frank's office. There, Frank had constructed a large metal box with a big red button on the top—big red buttons being a compulsory part of all science these days.

"Is that it?" Abilius asked.

"I know. I know. It should have far more in the way of wires, glowing panels and things, but it just didn't seem to need them," Frank explained. "Frankly, I'm not even sure why I linked the whole thing up to a BRB. It's just a metal box full of books that we open once a critical plot mass has been achieved."

"And has it?" Abilius asked.

"Probably. Did you decide-"

Abilius didn't even bother answering. Instead, he brought a hand down firmly on the big red button. The door swung open, and the two waited.

Nothing happened. Nothing continued to happen.

Abilius looked over at Frank. "Are you sure you got enough thrillers in there?"

"Pretty much everything they had in the university bookshop. Maybe if we-"

"Stop where you are!" A dozen figures in black clothes burst into the room, holding automatic weapons. Abilius and Frank put their hands up quickly. They'd had enough practice over the years. One of the newcomers stepped forwards. "Step away from the box so that my colleagues can seal it. We can't have anyone trying to stop the spread of normality. The fate of the world could be at stake."

Abilius stepped away from the box. He hadn't seen that one coming. What kind of group would be interested in something like this? More to the point, should he do as the figures said, even though it might mean never undoing the effect? How badly did he want things back to normal? Badly enough to take on trained military personnel who just happened to have… oh, of course.

"Frank," he said, "put your fingers in your ears."

Frank had the sense not to argue, thankfully, so when the package Abilius had thrown away so neatly exploded outside, they weren't deafened too badly. They even had enough of their wits about them to dive out of the second-floor window, while the special forces types started shooting one another by accident, landing on a crash mat the university's cheerleading squad just happened to be carrying below. As they hit it, Abilius smiled.

It was good to have things back the way they should be.

End

Between them, Reg and Cindy made quite a lot of phone calls over the next twenty minutes. They called a couple of blokes Reg knew who dabbled in the trade, but they didn't have any answers. They called one of the professors from the university where Cindy sat in on classes, but he didn't believe that what was happening was possible, or that it would be happening under a bucket if it were. They even tried calling the General Operating Division helpline, to see if they knew what to do, but after the first ten minutes of being put on hold, they gave up.

In mild desperation, they tried calling the police, who didn't really understand most of the ensuing conversation, but did at least send around a man from the bomb squad, wearing all the armor that made them look so much like baseball catchers. He took a look under the bucket, whistled, and hurried both Reg and Cindy out of the shed.

"Um… the thing is…" he began.

Reg sighed. "The thing is that it isn't technically a bomb, and that you don't have a clue how to disarm it, right?"

The man nodded. "Sorry. I guess I could evacuate the area, or put up some police tape, or something."

"And that would help when it blew up, would it?" Reg asked.

"Um… probably not." The man gave the shed a glum look. Reg was used to that. Mrs. Reg gave his shed some very glum looks indeed sometimes, mostly at times when Reg had just tracked grease into the house. This one seemed a little more serious though, and probably had a lot to do with the shed's role as a source of potentially impending doom. Not that tracking grease into Mrs. Reg's kitchen didn't signal potentially impending doom, but this doom wasn't just confined to the person doing the tracking.

"Could we maybe move the universe?" Cindy asked.

"How?" Reg asked. "It would only burn through any ropes we tried to attach to it, and I'm not picking it up. Besides, where would we put it?"

"I was thinking that we could maybe fly it out to sea or something and drop it there, where it wouldn't do any damage."

"Fly it out to sea?" Reg repeated. "We can't even touch it. Honestly, this is going to be like Burt Theakston's prize pumpkins all over again." He thought for a moment. "Except that even those only destroyed the allotments."

"I was thinking we could scoop it up in the coal bucket," Cindy suggested. "I mean, it hasn't burnt its way through yet."

"Even if you can though, how would we move it?" Reg folded his arms. "I'm not taking it on the bus. I had enough trouble with that wardrobe Vera bought that time."

"Actually," Cindy said, "I was thinking that this lovely man could maybe phone for a helicopter."

Cindy had a very persuasive smile, Reg had to admit. In less than two minutes, the young man from the bomb squad was explaining to his superiors exactly why he needed air support—although it might also have had something to do with the size of the potential explosion. They said it would be about another ten minutes, which was a bit worrying for Reg. Not so much because he suspected that the universe might go critical in that time, but more so because, at this rate, he was going to have to explain to Mrs. Reg why he was late home. Maybe it might be better to let the thing blow up after all—at least that would be quick.

In fact, the helicopter arrived in something closer to five minutes, although it did take the three of them a little longer to manhandle the coal bucket out of the shed while keeping the universe underneath, like a spider trapped under a glass. In a quick movement, Reg and the young man from the bomb squad upended the bucket, scooping the universe up neatly for at least a tenth of a second before it dropped straight through the bottom to crash to the floor.

"There's a hole in your bucket," Cindy observed. "And I don't think mending it is going to work..." Nor, from the looks of it, was much else.

The universe was about half buried in the ground thanks to the fall, but even like that, Reg could tell that it was bigger than it had been. He didn't have any theories to cover expanding universes and what they might do, but it probably wasn't a good sign.

It was almost as bad a sign, in fact, as the arrival of a couple of TV reporters. Reg didn't know where they'd come from. He and Alf had debated that one, and he was of the opinion that they were just another of those things that occasionally showed up in universes, no matter how carefully you tried to avoid them. They tried to ask

Reg's opinion on whether the world was about to be blown up before Cindy took charge of them, explaining that no, it wasn't going to be the world, just the universe. Oh, and about twenty square miles, so they might want to hurry up and get out of there. They stayed, of course, because you couldn't get good enough pictures of the destruction of things from twenty miles away, and because their studios had told them to—oh, and also because Cindy was a bit more photogenic than Reg and was happy to talk to them.

Reg was slightly less happy, because the universe was behaving in a very worrying way. It had stopped glowing yellow. Now, it was burning white hot and doing his leeks no good at all.

"Do you think it would help to pour water on it?" the man from the bomb squad asked. "You know, to cool it down?"

"Probably not—although I suppose we could all do with a nice cup of tea."

"And it's going to explode, isn't it?"

Reg shrugged. "I don't know. I think so."

"And there's nothing that you could think of that might work. We could hit it with-"

"We tried that. It didn't help."

"Oh."

Briefly, Reg wondered if he should wander back to be with Mrs. Reg. After all, there didn't seem to be much else he could do, and he was fairly sure that was the sort of thing you were meant to do at times of impending doom—that or find a suitable deity to pray to. Although in Reg's experience, most of them didn't understand enough about universe building to help. That was why they went to people like Reg and Alf.

That all meant that there was really only one thing left to do. With the sort of reluctance that Reg normally reserved only for visiting Mrs. Reg's sister, he asked to borrow a cell phone from one of the journalists, rang Alf, and explained what was going on.

"You daft bugger," Alf swore as Reg explained. "Right, don't touch anything. I'll be right over."

And he was. Ordinarily, it took Alf all his time to get anywhere, but in this case, it took him something less than three minutes to show up at the shed, riding on the back of Mrs. Orpington's mobility scooter and hopping off when he got close. He didn't say anything to Reg as he approached. Instead, he knelt beside the universe, examining it closely.

"This is the girl's doing, is it?" Alf asked after a bit.

"She didn't know any better," Reg said. "She was doing fine until then."

Alf nodded. "Aye, I imagine she was. Where is she?"

Reg shrugged. Cindy had wandered off with the nice young bomb disposal man a little while before, presumably to do the kind of thing people traditionally did when their destruction seemed imminent. Ah, young love. Well, young something, anyway.

"You couldn't ring me before?" Alf demanded, with another look at the universe.

Reg looked at his shoes. "Sorry, Alf. It's bad then?"

"Of course it's bad," Alf said. "It's far too far gone to do anything about now."

"Oh."

Somehow, Reg hadn't imagined it being like that. He'd imagined that ringing Alf would somehow sort it all out. Alf always knew best, even if his welding wasn't up to much these days. Reg had assumed that he would have had a second safety backup or that he would know of some way of cooling universes, involving nothing more than a couple of bags of frozen peas and Reg's second-best flat cap. That he didn't meant that it was over. They were going to die. They were actually going to die.

"So that's it then?"

"Yes," Alf said. "Which is a bloody annoyance. I mean, all the work we've put into this one, and now it's gone critical. That's the last thing we need."

"Yes," Reg agreed. "Plus it's probably going to kill everyone for miles around."

"Oh, they hardly ever do that these days—especially not when they're young."

"What?"

"Mostly, they just fly off and bother sheep. Or is it worry them? I never get that right. Still, it's what people want, so-"

"Alf?"

"Yes, Reg?"

"What are you talking about?"

Alf didn't answer, but instead took a small silver tuning fork from his pocket. He tapped it experimentally against a rock. "Does that sound like E flat to you? Has to be E flat to work. Oh, well, it's the only one I've got, so it had better be."

He tapped the tuning fork against the white-hot outer skin of the universe. Amazingly, it didn't melt, nor did his arm. Instead, the universe rang with the sound of the fork, resonating with it perfectly.

"E flat," Cindy said, wandering up and adjusting her boiler suit as she did so.

"I thought you'd gone off with that young man," Reg said.

Cindy shrugged. "For a guy who works with bombs, he's not very patient. What's happening?"

Reg didn't have an answer to that as the universe continued to ring. It rang and rang, growing in volume, until Reg had to cover his ears. It rang, and it stretched, and parts of its outer layer fell away. As it did, it occurred to Reg that there was one very obvious word for a round object with lots of stuff inside it, separated from the world by a thin shell.

That word was "egg".

The skin of the universe fell away, revealing a different sort of skin. This skin was scaly, and green, and still glowing faintly with heat. It belonged to a small, lizard-like creature with what could only be described as wings sticking up from its back. It took a faltering step forward and sneezed, shooting a jet of flame out over the shed.

"Hang on," Reg said. "What's going on? Why do we have *dragons* coming out of our universe?"

Alf looked at him like he'd just asked why the sky was blue (to which the answer was generally "because of the blu-tack" in the case of those worlds made by the pair).

"Well, what *else* did you think they were for?"

Reg didn't really have an answer to that, so he, along with Cindy, a couple of news crews, and a rather embarrassed looking bomb disposal expert without most of his protective clothing, spent the next few seconds watching the small reptile that had come out of the universe stretch its wings, flap them once, and take to the air like a rocket.

"You never told me about that bit," Cindy said as it left.

Reg shook his head. "I didn't know. I… didn't know."

Apparently, the film crews didn't either, because they wandered off, trying to work out exactly who they should be sending the footage to, and whether Attenborough was doing anything at the moment. The man from the bomb squad left with his friends in the helicopter, which set off in roughly the direction the dragon had gone.

For several seconds after that, Alf, Reg, and Cindy were quiet.

Then Alf harrumphed. "What are you two standing there for? We've got work to do, you know."

"Work?" Cindy asked. "You want me to help?"

"I don't see that I've got much choice," Alf replied, "though Reg reckons you did all right. Fact is, thanks to the two of you, we've now have a week in which to deliver one fully functional bespoke universe."

Reg's eyebrows beetled together. "A week? Can we even do it in that?"

Alf shrugged. "It's not like we've got much choice now, is it? Anyway, there's three of us if the girl helps out." He looked at Cindy. "You still want to help out?"

Cindy nodded. "Absolutely. But a week…"

"So it won't be the best job we've ever done," Alf said. "Still, I reckon we can throw *something* together."

If You Can't Behead Them...

Noah had been ready for the zombie apocalypse for months when it happened. Well, you had to be ready for these things, didn't you? The signs were obvious, and it wasn't like there was a lack of information around on what you needed to do. You needed to stock up on food, stay indoors, learn how to use a machete properly, and be very careful not to let anyone in who is talking about brains. Easy.

Practically the same stuff he'd already learnt to deal with the possibility of a sudden nuclear war, or the imminent breakdown of all governmental structures, when you thought about it. It was practically the kind of thing he did for fun, even if it wasn't the kind of thing other eighteen-year-old boys did for fun. Noah would have done the kind of things that other eighteen-year-old boys considered to be fun too, except that girls never seemed to find the prospect of an impending zombie apocalypse interesting, and his grandmother, with whom he lived, always got so upset if he went out partying.

So he stayed home and learned to use a machete instead. Noah learned to use it over the internet, practicing on watermelons until he was pretty sure he could stop any zombie stupid enough to come to his house. It was amazing what you could learn over the internet these days. There were guys out there who could teach you to kill a man with a single touch, apparently. However, that kind of thing probably didn't work on zombies, so Noah hadn't bothered learning it.

He learned everything else, though, so on the day the dead rose, he'd been more than ready. He pushed his grandmother back into the house, barricaded them inside, and waited for the shambling hordes to do their worst. Of course, she hadn't been happy about that, because she always went to her book group on Thursdays, but Noah had insisted.

They stayed like that for more than two weeks, watching the news, waiting for it to be over—well, mostly waiting for the zombies to just try breaking in so that he could give them a taste of cold steel, in Noah's case, but waiting, nonetheless. Even when there was no immediate rampaging or brain eating, Noah insisted that they should wait, just in case the zombies were lulling them all into a false sense of security or something. They only came out when Noah's grandmother insisted that it was stupid waiting around inside like that, and that in any case, she wasn't going to subsist on a diet of baked beans on toast any longer, thank you very much.

For the month after that, Noah watched the news some more, every night after getting back from school and his job at the local garage. He checked into internet forums on zombies, and got quite excited when he saw stories of them being a secret army of evil, before he realized that the forums in question also thought that Hispanics, Asians, and practically everyone else was part of the same army. Noah couldn't imagine Mr. Chen two houses down being part of a secret army of evil.

Gradually, Noah came to the same inescapable conclusion as the rest of the country: zombies were boring. They just shuffled about, got on with things, and didn't say very much at all. They certainly never said, "Braaaiiins!" The closest that they came to it was that some of them seemed to quite like semolina pudding, which some of the people on TV said looked a bit like brains, though Noah couldn't see it, himself.

Mostly though, they just got jobs. Zombies didn't want to be paid much, and they didn't get distracted, so pretty quickly, all kinds of people hired them. Some people complained that too many people hired them, given that there weren't enough jobs to go around. Noah wasn't one of them, at first, not even when Mr. Lafferty at the shop got a couple of zombies in to do overnight work on cars. Mostly, that just confirmed how boring zombies were to Noah.

The rest of the undead weren't much better. Vampires turned out to be an occasional problem for the school system, but mostly they weren't interested in biting people. One of the girls in Noah's class *said* that she'd been bitten, but Noah was pretty sure she'd done the marks herself, with lipstick. She had a friend, named Moira, who liked that Noah knew about zombies—liked it enough that she let him take her to the movies a couple of times, but not enough to let him kiss her.

For almost a month, Noah had no problems with zombies. He told himself that they were just grey, shuffling people, the way everyone else did, and that they weren't so bad. After all, he'd never had a problem with accountants. Then Mr. Lafferty declared that there wasn't enough work to go around at the shop and that he was going to have to let Noah go. Noah tried looking for work, but when people found out that he would want to stop to do things like eat and sleep, he didn't get the jobs.

Moira left him after a week. She'd liked what Noah knew about zombies, she said, but she had decided to find out more about them for herself. Specifically, she had decided to find out more about a zombie by the name of Jimmy, who lived down by the river. When Noah complained, she told him to get a life, which seemed a bit unfair, really, given her current choice of boyfriend.

Noah went back to sitting inside with the door locked after that, staying that way for more than a day. He briefly went back to the forums he'd been on before, and he started to wonder whether he should get out his baseball bat and machete, since obviously, zombies were a lot more dangerous than people thought.

In the end, though, he didn't. He went to the library instead. He went to a few other corners of the internet. He went to a little old voodoo woman who lived downtown, whose business was booming. She told him what he needed. She even sold him most of it, adding on sales tax and putting it in a paper bag. When Noah got home, he cooked it up on the stove and drank the resulting green sludge down. It didn't seem to make any difference.

So he went out to look for work again, shuffling his way down to the docks. He shuffled into the manager's office, and tried to explain what he wanted, but he couldn't figure out how to put it into words, so he just groaned instead. When he groaned, Noah looked at his reflection in the nearest window and smiled—not happily, exactly, but at least with some satisfaction. The way he saw it, if you couldn't beat them, then you might as well join them.

The Last Drop

They came to O'Connell's Auction House in their ones and twos, scuttling their way across the city, arriving by electric car, solar glider, hydrogen limousine, and kite-powered land yacht. A few even showed up by bicycle, with their bodyguards pedaling along furiously behind—or in front, in the case of one dowager duchess on a tandem.

They needed bodyguards because they were rich. Actually, they were more than rich—rich enough that the merely rich seemed like they were flipping burgers by comparison; rich enough that a zero here and there at the end of a bank balance ceased to have much real meaning; rich enough that, ordinarily, they would never have condescended to come to a simple auction. They came today, though.

That meant, as Andrew O'Connell stood behind his rostrum, looking out over the assembled crowd, he had to work quite hard not to run away. You didn't get a crowd like this when you were selling, for example, a collection of late twenty-first century training shoes, or some early Wedgewood, or a selection of largely obsolete computers. Although, maybe if he had been selling any of those things, he wouldn't have been quite so nervous.

What he *was* selling sat in a small glass vial on the rostrum, stared at the whole time by two security guards. Each one was big enough to block out the light if he got too close, and the overall effect of having one on either side was a bit like being a butterfly being pressed between two heavy books. Andrew put up with it. He could put up with a lot, given the amount of money involved in today's auction.

All this for a drop of oil—the last one. The last of anything was valuable, but it wasn't exactly a Picasso, was it?

Not that Andrew could label it as the last drop, not officially anyway. In theory, the oil wells that had been dry for twenty years now might crank out another barrel tomorrow; or someone might find half a gallon in the tank of a rusting Mini Cooper out in the desert; or some strange old man might turn up, having stockpiled a tanker's worth in Tupperware in his attic. Even if one didn't, there were still biodiesels to think about; "oils" that had about as much to do with the real stuff as flat pack furniture had to do with Chippendale, in Andrew's opinion, but the law probably thought differently.

Yet, realistically, it was the last drop. People had stopped using petrol powered cars a hundred years back, when the cost of them finally got to be too much. Industries had switched over to alternatives, and even race cars were mostly powered by the motoring equivalent of big elastic bands wound up really tight these days. Although admittedly, it didn't do much for the lap records. Scarcity and prices had forced people to do what merely being told they were ruining their own planet couldn't. Then the oil had finally run out—which left this: the last honest to goodness petroleum anywhere—the end of an era. That was certainly what the newspapers were calling it, and if Andrew had carefully denied it when they put that to him, that was only because he had a pretty good idea of what happened when people went around denying things to newspapers.

Yesterday, for example, the headline on his flat screen reader had said: "Officially Not the Last Oil!" This meant that they'd then had to spend almost a full page explaining why that was technically the case, complete with testimony from a couple of professors, an interview with the current head of Greenpeace, saying why it was a good thing, and some carefully printed details of where the auction was taking place that the newspaper had somehow found out. Andrew had to repeat that bit to them twice before they got O'Connell down correctly.

Oh, well. It was probably time to get it over with—if becoming obscenely rich on the commission was something to be gotten over with.

Andrew banged his gavel on the rostrum. "Ladies and gentlemen, welcome to O'Connell's Auction House. If you'd like to finish taking your seats, we can get on with the sale."

A couple of sheiks elbowed one another out of the way in an effort to get the last chair. Andrew waited just long enough to smirk before speaking again.

"Now, we have just the one lot for you today, but I think you'll all agree that it's a special one. In any case, it means we all get to go home early."

That got a tiny titter of laughter from the auction crowd, which just went to show how nervous some of them were too as Andrew tried to spin things out a bit. He wasn't used to the idea of a single lot. Every auctioneer's instinct he had told him that it wasn't the way you did things. If you had an item like this, then what you did, if you had any sense, was to get a bunch of other things—things that you generally had a hard time shifting because there weren't enough rich idiots in the room—and you put them in on the one occasion when there would be.

Andrew had overruled that instinct. Having other lots today would be… well, it would be a bit like having an orchestra in to play Bach, and then insisting that it warm up with the greatest hits of the Wurzels. In any case, he didn't want to think about what might happen if the vial currently sitting on his rostrum were there long enough to evaporate in the heat of the day. That was the kind of thought to give Andrew's accountant a heart attack, and it wasn't doing him much good either.

"Now, you all know what this is," Andrew said, nodding to the vial, "so where should we open the bidding?" He read the figure he was supposed to start at off a card, because his head refused to believe that anyone would go for it. "Will anyone start me at a hundred thousand dollars?"

A computer magnate, a business tycoon, and one of the sheiks all raised hands so fast it was a wonder sheer air friction didn't set their sleeves on fire.

"A hundred and ten. A hundred and twenty."

The two sheiks made the early running, although Andrew got the feeling they were doing that mostly because they knew they couldn't afford to make the later running, and they wanted to be seen to take an interest. There wasn't as much money in oil-sheiking as there had been, after all.

Andrew shifted to twenty-five thousand dollar increments after two hundred thousand. At a quarter of a million dollars, one sheik dropped out, to be replaced by a computer magnate who had made his money realizing that what people really want from their computers is something to blame when things go wrong, and who had installed more bugs in each model to give them an excuse. He went as high as four hundred thousand.

The other sheik was long gone by then, being replaced by the dowager duchess and then an Iowa biodiesel magnate, who presumably wanted it for the nostalgia value. After all, fields of oil seed rape and large vats of genetically modified algae probably weren't quite the same.

He hung in until they passed the million mark, and then the serious players jumped in. One, the heir to quite a large shipping line and quite a small hotel chain, thanks to him being allowed to run the latter but not the former, pushed on quickly, obviously trying to muscle the opposition out of the bidding. The other, a young woman in a dark t-shirt and jeans, which looked so scruffy they had either been bought from a charity shop or cost a fortune, kept pace.

They went up past two million so fast that Andrew was convinced he had blacked out for a moment. Things slowed a little as they got past two and a half, but then picked up again as the shipping heir tried to project confidence. The young woman just kept bidding. As they crept up still higher, Andrew could see the shipping heir shaking.

"The bid stands a three million, nine hundred thousand," Andrew said at last. "Will you go to four million, sir?"

The heir was on the phone, presumably to whoever it was he was actually heir to. From the looks of it, the conversation wasn't going well.

"I have to ask again," Andrew said. "Will you go to four million?"

"Will you take three nine fifty?"

"Three million, nine hundred and fifty thousand is bid."

"Four million," the young woman said promptly.

Andrew looked back at the shipping heir, but they all knew what they would see. Without looking at Andrew, the man shook his head. Andrew looked around. "Four million one hundred thousand, anyone?"

Silence.

"Last time of asking. The bid stands at four million dollars. Do we have any more bids?" Andrew waited a second, then brought his gavel down. "Sold."

A ripple went through the room. The young woman in the dark t-shirt stood up, approaching the front. Nobody moved as she made an electronic transfer to the auction house. They all just watched her.

"So… um…" Andrew began. He wasn't normally tongue tied, but the sight of millions of dollars coming into his company accounts could do a lot to a man. "What do you plan on doing with your purchase?"

"Doing?" the young woman smiled. It wasn't an unpleasant smile. "How many things are there to do with oil?"

Andrew looked out over his auction crowd. At a guess, he'd have said that roughly fifty percent would have stuck it in a cooled vault somewhere, twenty percent would have donated it to a gallery, another twenty percent would have kept it on their desk, while ten percent would probably have used it to fuel about thirty seconds of chainsaw use.

"I'm going to do the only thing you can do with the last drop of oil," the woman said.

"What's that?"

She smiled again, looking round at the rest of the room. Still, no one had left their seat. "I own it now? It's legally mine, to do with as I wish?"

Andrew nodded.

The woman picked up the vial. Very slowly, obviously aware that people were watching her, she poured it out onto the floor before moving back a step or two. Just as deliberately, she took a box of matches out of her pocket and lit one.

"Good."

Is Nigh

"Henry Larman?" the young woman who walked into his bar asked. Henry didn't bother saying anything stupid like "who wants to know" or "I might be." Either you were somebody, or you weren't.

Given that the young woman was a pretty thing of about twenty, with flowing blonde hair and a dress that strongly suggested she wasn't some kind of process server, if only because it didn't give her anywhere to stow legal documents, Henry decided that he probably was somebody tonight.

"That's me."

"Oh. Good." The young lady hesitated. "Now, I've got to be sure to get this right. How was I supposed to say it? Oh, yes. Henry Larman, the end of the world is nigh."

"That so?" Henry picked up a glass and started polishing it, more out of habit than with any actual expectation that the thing would end up clean.

"Um, you did hear me correctly, didn't you?" The young woman moved closer. Henry didn't have a problem with that. "I mean, I might have messed up the enunciation, what with all the declaiming."

"You said that the end of the world was near, right?"

"Nigh. Not near. Nigh."

"Thought that was what horses did."

"That's neigh."

Henry put the glass down. "The end of the world is neigh? Sister, you're making less sense than you did when you first came in."

The woman put her hands on her hips. "You're making fun of me. I'm telling you that the end of the world is nigh, and you're making fun of me."

Henry shrugged. "A bit. You got a name?"

"Cassariel. You can call me Cassie."

Henry nodded, got out a bottle of beer, and put it down on the bar. Cassie sat down and stared at it.

"What's this?"

"It's beer. Look, you haven't sold me the whole end of the world line, so you really aren't going to persuade me that you've never heard of beer."

Cassie opened the bottle, took a sip of the contents, and made a face. "Are you trying to tell me that people actually drink this stuff?"

"In quite large quantities. Now, are you going to tell me what's really going on?" Henry asked. "Or am I going to have to call the cops?"

"But I've *told* you," Cassie insisted. "The end of the world is nigh. How much clearer do you want me to be?"

Henry sighed. "Look, the way I see it, you're either crazy or selling something. Are you selling something?"

Cassie shook her head.

"I didn't think so. So you're crazy, but it's not like I care. Half the people who come in here are crazy. So how about we don't say any more about the end of the world, you have a few drinks, and then you go home to wherever you go?"

"But-"

Apparently, it wasn't going to be that easy. "Look," Henry said, "I'm really not interested."

"How can you not be interested? The world is coming to an end."

"Really? When?"

"A week from Tuesday," Cassie replied. "Your time, it would be about half past seven at night. You know, give or take."

"Give or take." Henry sighed. "Right, that does it. Get out, please."

"You're throwing me out?" Cassie looked hurt.

"What did you expect? Besides, we're not even meant to be open right now."

"Oh." Cassie stood up. She looked back at her beer for a moment, picked it up, and drank it down. She made another face. "Urrgh! Does that stuff ever grow on you? No, don't answer that."

She stood there a moment longer, and then she started to glow. She glowed with an inner light that seemed to grow and grow, building moment by moment until Henry couldn't look straight at her anymore.

"Hey, what are you…" he didn't finish that. Mostly because, as the afterimages faded, he realized that he was talking to an empty bar. For several seconds, Henry just stared at the spot Cassie had occupied. Then he stared at the ceiling. "This doesn't mean I believe you, you know!"

On the first day after the angel appeared to him, Henry didn't open the bar. Mostly because, after about lunchtime, he was too busy drinking the contents. On the second day, he did, if only to show people that he wouldn't be intimidated. Exactly whom he was showing, Henry wasn't entirely certain. Late on the afternoon of the second day, Henry mentioned what had happened to a couple of his regulars, in a "hey, can you believe the stupid things that happen to me" kind of way. They laughed.

The guy from the TV studio sitting at the next table didn't laugh. He was too busy putting a call through to his boss. Well, it had been a very slow week, as far as news was concerned, and it had been *ages* since they'd had anyone claiming that the world was about to end. The guy's boss thought he was crazy, but agreed that yes, it might do a lot to fill that slot on the nightly news where they had been planning an interview with a soon-to-be jailed recording artist, before that artist rather thoughtlessly absconded to Mexico without telling them.

That was how, on the third day, Henry ended up explaining what had happened to a TV studio audience. He did his best to just stick to the facts of what had happened, but the interviewer kept asking his opinion on things. Henry had plenty of opinions. After all, bars ran on opinions as much as on beer. By the end of it, even he was sure he knew why the apocalypse was coming and what they all should have done differently—although he didn't close down his bar.

By the end of the weekend, people were flocking round, taking pictures of Henry at work. They didn't buy as many drinks as Henry would have liked, but then he guessed that he wasn't going to have much to spend the money on in a few days anyway. People came around in packs when he left the bar, wanting to know how they could be among the ones saved from the end. Henry had to tell them that he didn't know, and that he was closing the bar on the Monday.

On the second to the last Monday, Henry went to visit his sister. He didn't visit much, because he never liked the way his sister asked him when he was going to stop tending bar and get a real job. This time, he wasn't sure what he was going to say. She wasn't particularly interested in the end of the world, since her loser of a boyfriend had run off again, but she did at least say that it had been funny to see Henry on TV.

He came back on Tuesday to find that, in his absence, people had come out to declare that what he was saying was nonsense. The public leaders pointed out that there was no history of apocalypses happening on their watch, and they weren't about to start now. The TV evangelists said that it couldn't be the end of the world in a week's time, because they knew when it was the end of the world, and it wasn't then. And incidentally, people ought to send them money if they wanted to be absolutely certain.

By about Thursday, people were calling Henry a fraud and a cheat. They were claiming that he was out to bilk them of their money, and that he was the father of their unborn children. Henry was pretty certain that he wasn't. A few people came out in his defense, gathering round the bar and chanting slogans, asking Henry for his guidance until he told them all to go home.

The weekend was pretty quiet, giving Henry plenty of time to think. He called a couple of old friends. Most of them couldn't remember who he was. On the last Monday, he sold everything he had, from the bar down to his old clothes, to anyone who was passing, for anything they would pay. He spent the night sitting on a park bench, staring at the stars. It was cold, but Henry didn't care. He'd never just watched the stars before, and if he'd seen the dawn, it was normally in a bleary haze, not sharp and red and rising.

He spent the day on Tuesday not knowing what to do. He thought about doing all kinds of things; things he hadn't done, and things he'd done so much they'd become like habits. Instead, he walked. He walked around the city, taking in a soup kitchen where he left the money he'd made from selling his things. He must have walked in a circle, because by the early evening, he'd arrived back at the bench. Well, that was good enough.

Henry sat down. He waited. Occasionally, he checked his watch. When it got to half past seven, he stood up and looked around. The world seemed to still be there. Well, that was that then.

"Hello, Henry."

Cassie was there when he turned around.

"You."

"You've cost me almost five dollars, you know. I had my money on you going on some kind of rampage." She held out a bottle of beer. It appeared to be one of the ones from Henry's former bar. "But you have introduced me to this stuff, so I guess it works out."

Henry ran that through his head. "This was all some kind of test? You wanted to see what I would do?"

Cassie shrugged. "Obviously."

"And the world isn't going to end really, is it?" Henry tried to get angry, but he found that he was just tired. There would be so many things to do tomorrow, and the next day…

"That kind of depends on whether we're talking about the general or the specific, Henry."

"What?"

"Well, if you're asking whether the whole world is ending, for everyone, then the answer is no. That's the general sense. The specific, on the other hand… look around, Henry."

Henry Larman looked around. There, on the bench, he saw the form of Henry Larman. It looked very still.

"Oh."

"Oh, indeed," Cassie said, hooking an arm through his.

"So what happens now?" Henry asked.

Cassie told him.

Henry nodded. "Well, that's all right then."

A Losing Hand

The problem with people, Verrain knew, as he sat at the card table, was that they never knew when to quit. They never knew when to get up, walk out, and get on with their lives—not that he was complaining, exactly. People who didn't know when to quit kept his little game in business, kept it earning—earning enough for Verrain to have a nice suit and an expensive haircut, a watch that had once belonged to a prince down on his luck, and shoes that had formerly been owned by a would-be sharp who'd tried to push his.

He earned other things too, because that was the rule here. That was what made Verrain's game more than just some backstreet card school. That was what made the fish and the sharks come in and what *kept* them coming in. At Verrain's game, you could bet what you liked, when you liked. No limit. No *limits*. You could bet your shirt or your grandmother, half an hour's time at a theatre next Wednesday, or twenty years of your life. Verrain hadn't stayed looking twenty-eight for three hundred years by turning down bets like that. Though there were days… no, it was good. It was all good.

Of course, it meant he had to keep things moving, too. You couldn't stay in one spot too long, even with a regular game. With one like this… well, he'd set up in the back rooms of clubs and the front rooms of country houses, on top of Ayres Rock and on the flight decks of an aging aircraft carrier—anywhere there was someone to play and anywhere word could get out, in those strange, ineffable ways that word always got out about the game. Occasionally, Verrain would wonder what those ways were; he certainly didn't have anything to do with them.

Tonight his little table was tucked into a lock up near London's second most famous bridge: the rebuilt one. It was just a little homage to the time an American had bet him that bridge, and had then had to go and buy it, brick by brick, when he had lost. There had been a couple of players in the early evening, nothing players, betting a few thousand dollars here, a year or two there—enough to warm up with, but not enough to make the trip worthwhile and not enough to make it interesting, but hardly anything did, these days.

Things got a little better as the evening wore on. A woman, who lost more money than she should have, offered Verrain an hour of her time the next night on one hand, trying to win it back. She lost that too. A professor from the British Museum tried to win that hour off Verrain, and promptly lost two priceless La Tene culture swords. Verrain wondered how he was going to cover up their loss. But then, he'd heard somewhere that the British Museum had so many artifacts that they had to keep them hidden away in movable shelves, so maybe they would be grateful for the room. He didn't particularly care.

At midnight, two more players drifted in. Were they there together? No, Verrain could no more imagine this pair knowing one another than he could imagine himself not playing. One was sharply dressed, with silver cufflinks, slicked back hair, the whole bit—a "player", in other words, or at least someone who liked to think that they were. The other was badly shaven, lank haired, and looked like he hadn't changed his clothes in a day or two. They were both about twenty-five, but if they had arrived together, it was only because one had waited outside until the other arrived, too scared to go in alone. They sat down at the table at almost the same time.

"The game is poker, gentlemen," Verrain said. "Hold'em. No limit, of course." He didn't bother smiling at his own little joke. He'd said it too many times. Of the two men, the slick one smiled; the other didn't. "Just call out what you want to bet, and I'll decide what it's worth. You see your cards, then you bet or you fold."

He dealt the first few cards. The slick man pulled out a briefcase. It had diamonds in it. Predictable enough. Verrain examined them and nodded. "So you're betting one briefcase of legitimate, uncut diamonds against… shall we say ten million?"

"Dollars?"

"Pounds. We are in London, after all. Do you accept?"

The slick man nodded. The other man, the one who wasn't dressed so well, folded before the betting. Verrain hoped he wouldn't be one of those who only showed up so he could say he had. Verrain hated those—almost as much as he hated one other thing. He dealt out the remainder of the cards. He won, of course. The man in the sharp suit started to push over the case with an exaggerated sigh.

"Why are you doing that?" Verrain asked.

"The deal was-"

"For a case full of real diamonds, not the fakes you have there." Verrain smiled faintly as he watched that sink in, then handed over a card. "You have until noon tomorrow to deposit them with this solicitor. You know what will happen if you are late."

The man blanched.

"Unless you would like to try to win them back? We could play for… shall we say a year per million's worth of stones?"

He barely even considered it before leaving. Verrain snorted. Not just a cheat, but a coward too. He looked over at the other man. "And are you going to actually play a hand tonight?"

The man swallowed, then nodded. Verrain dealt four cards—two to each of them. Verrain shrugged and dealt out two cards to each of them. His face didn't betray a flicker of emotion as he checked his to find two aces. But then, he'd schooled his face not to give anything away a hundred years before.

"And what will you bet?"

"Everything."

Verrain raised an eyebrow. "Define everything."

The other man shrugged. "My name. My life. Everything I own. Everything I am."

Despite himself, Verrain was impressed. "All on this hand?"

"Yes."

Verrain thought for a moment. "No one has bet that before."

"I guessed they hadn't."

"And against that, shall we say-"

"One week."

Again, Verrain found himself faintly surprised. "You could ask for more. For everything, you could ask for a lot more. Once we agree, you can't change the bet."

The other man shrugged. "I know what the time is worth. One week."

Verrain nodded. "Agreed."

Then, for no good reason, the other man turned his hand over to reveal a two and a three.

"It isn't time for that yet," Verrain said, slightly annoyed. Did this man not know how to play?

"I know how the game goes." The man looked straight at Verrain for a moment. "Tell me, do you?"

"I think I do by now," Verrain said, and dealt the next card. A queen. He'd played a queen once, one of the faerie ones, and had won the keys to a forgotten kingdom. Had he ever done anything with them?

"Really? How about life? Do you know how that goes? I guess you don't see much outside of this game. Mind you, I can hardly talk. I haven't seen much outside of a hospital for the last six months."

"Ah," Verrain said, understanding. "A dying man then. How long?"

"I'm meant to be dead already. I figure that, to a man like that…"

"A week might be more than enough after all."

"Too late to change bets," the man said. "You said so yourself."

Verrain nodded. "I did."

He dealt a king to go with the queen. He'd played more than enough kings. He'd won English George's mind, and jewels from Rajas of the East. He'd won the peace of the kingdom from the French Louis, plunging the place into a revolution, and sold it to monks in Tibet.

"Do you ever get tired if it?" the other man asked, interrupting his thoughts.

"Tired of what?"

His opponent shrugged. "Life. The game. The endless taking."

Normally, Verrain would have laughed at that, but the cards were clear. The other man wouldn't be leaving the room. "Sometimes."

He dealt the final card: an eight. Not really enough of them to make a true dead man's hand, but it would do for tonight.

"And that's-"

"You still have to turn over your cards," the other man said, coughing. Verrain thought he saw a fleck or two of blood. "You have to show the hand to win, right? Unless you're planning to fold."

"Now why would I-" Verrain began, and stopped. "Is that what this is about? You thought I would hear your story and give away perfectly good time? Why would I do that?"

"Pity."

Verrain shook his head and flipped over his aces. "I don't have any. Or not enough to matter, anyway."

His opponent smiled a rictus grin. "I know, but I had to give you the chance."

"What are you… oh!" Verrain rocked as pain hit him. He looked down at his hands, watching as the skin began to become paper thin. "What did you do?"

The other man smiled. It was a very familiar smile. Verrain saw it in the mirror most mornings. "I just made a bet. You know, I had to wait a while for a cheat to show up, so you would think too hard about him, and not enough about that."

"What did you *do?*" Verrain repeated, his voice sounded different, somehow.

The other man shrugged, and it was Verrain's shrug. "You won everything I am. Of course, if you're taking that, then there's the question of what happens to everything *you* are."

He seemed to breathe in then, but it was more than that. It was like he pulled the space around him into himself, sucking it in and holding it, forcing it to settle. When he was done, it was like there were two Verrains sitting at the card table—except that there weren't, because the former Verrain could feel the other man's rough clothes on his back, could remember a name other than Verrain as his own, could feel the agony of his own body trying to kill him with cancer.

The Verrain across the table nodded. "I'll tell you what," he said. "I'll give you the week anyway."

A week? A week was nothing, not against the centuries he'd… hang on, what was he talking about? He hadn't lived centuries. Nobody did that. He'd lived thirty-five years, and he had a house an hour's drive away, with a kid, and a wife, and…

And put like that, one more week was a very long time indeed. He stood up, holding out a hand. "Thank you, sir. Thank you so much."

Across from him, Verrain stood up. "Believe me, it was my pleasure. Spend your week well."

"Believe me, I will."

Horsemen

I'm just closing up for the night when the messenger comes into the library I work in. Yes, I work in a library. Where would you work if you were an angel? You've got order, and peace, and the opportunity to help people. Admittedly, it's mostly the opportunity to help people find the book they really need, but sometimes that's enough, you know? And besides, you can go on all you want about my lot dancing on the head of a pin, but how many of us have really mastered the Dewey Decimal system?

Not that I dance anywhere much. I never really seem to have the right dresses for it. But that's beside the point. The point is that I'm just getting ready to go home when an angelic light shines down, and there's a man's voice.

"Lariazelle?"

"I normally go by Lara these days, but yes."

"You are hereby notified that the ultimate plan has been put into operation. Please be ready to fulfill your appointed role in the final reckoning one month from now. If you need to be reminded of your role in the final days, please contact your local supervisor."

With that, the light blinks out. I hate recorded messages.

I hate this one more than most, which probably counts as blasphemy. The end? Already? I've hardly been here… all right, so it's probably a thousand years now, maybe even two, but who's counting? Someone, apparently, and now they're counting *down.*

Damn it. Yes, I know an angel shouldn't use language like that. I think, under the circumstances, that I'm entitled.

My mood carries over into my next day at work. Angels shouldn't have bad moods, but I've been around humans long enough to pick up the habit. I'm a bit short with those library users who don't remember to stay quiet at the best of times, but today I glare at them in a way that would probably have them keeling over if there were any justice.

Of course, they'll be keeling over soon enough. That's not exactly a cheering thought.

I've just applied a library stamp to a returned book with enough force to make the desk shake, when Mandy, who helps out at the library, comes up to me. She's a petite little thing with hair whose color seems to vary from week to week and who has a tendency to wear too much black for her complexion, but she's probably one of the closer people to me here.

"Everything okay, Lara?"

"Sure. It's nothing." Or impending nothingness where the world used to be, anyway, followed by so much judging and sorting that it will make the days when all the older folk come in together to change their books look easy. I look at Mandy. I'm pretty sure that she'll end up on the right side of that sorting, and I know I should be happy that it's finally coming, but really, the thought of her dying along with everyone else isn't a nice one.

"It doesn't look like nothing."

And it's then that I realize what I've more or less known since the night before. I don't want this. I don't want the end of the world—which is a bit awkward, really, because I'm pretty sure that I don't get a say in it. One of the minor joys of a divine instruction is that there isn't really anyone to complain to if you don't like it. Bugger.

"Mandy," I ask, knowing that I shouldn't, but not really able to stop myself, "what would you do if you knew that everything was due to end?"

"What? You mean like someone closing the library? They aren't going to close the library, are they?"

"No, no," I say quickly. "This is just hypothetical." Well, it is—until next month, at least.

"You're sure? Because if they are, I'm getting a petition together right now, and then maybe we should strike or have a protest or something, and-"

I'm not listening. I'm too busy thinking. Could it be that simple? Would it work? Am I about to get myself into more trouble than I can possibly imagine? There's only one way to find out, I guess.

"Mandy," I say, "you're a genius."

The expression on her face as I disappear is, well, exactly what you'd expect from someone whose co-worker has just disappeared. Maybe, if I'm very lucky, I'll even get to explain it to her.

It takes me most of a day to find War. What can I say? He gets around a lot these days—mostly to places where I have to spend a lot of time ducking. I mean, yes, technically bullets aren't going to kill me, but I'm going to look a bit stupid dropping into one of Heaven's workshops for repairs so soon before the big push. I'd probably even have to answer questions.

I finally find War in the stands of a hockey game. His current form is that of a burly man in his twenties, eating a hotdog, and yelling down at the players with the rest of the fans.

"Go on, kill him! Honestly man, do you not know how to use a stick properly?"

Out on the ice, a fight breaks out. I sit down next to him.

"War?"

"Who are you?"

"Lara. I'm-"

"I know *what* you are," War says, staring down at the ice. "Oh, come on. Is that any way to pull someone's shirt over his head?"

"I wanted to talk to you about…" I look round at all the humans there. They probably won't care much about anything I say, but I'm a librarian. Shouting things out isn't exactly in my nature. "About what's going to happen next month."

War looks at me for the first time. Really looks. "If you can't remember what you're meant to be doing, then I suggest you talk to your supervisor."

"I know what I'm meant to be doing," I say. "It's just…" here comes the bit that will get me into trouble. "I don't want to do it."

There's a goal. War ignores it, staring at me. "What? No, wait, we need somewhere we can talk." He takes hold of my arm, and a second later we're in a bunker somewhere. "I thought I just heard you say that you didn't want to do your job in the last days."

I shrug. "That's because I said it."

"You do realize that I ought to report you just for saying that kind of thing?"

"But you haven't," I point out. "You could have done it instantly. All I'm saying is... well, why does the world have to end so soon?"

War shrugs. "It's the ineffable plan. You can't go around trying to understand it. That's what it *means*."

"I know," I say, "but you can't think it's right."

War looks at me carefully. "Why are you doing this?" he asks. "What do you want?"

"I'm doing this because I like humans," I say. I take a breath. "And I think you do too."

"Like them?" War laughs. It's a long, rumbling laugh, like a series of cluster bombs going off. "I spend my life trying to get them to kill one another."

"And what other species does that so readily?" I demand. "Humans are so inventive when they kill one another. I saw you at that game. You like watching them."

"Well," War admits, "they have been doing some very interesting things with hunter/killer drones and long-range missiles recently."

"But they won't be doing that anymore after the end, will they? You won't have anyone to watch. You won't be relevant."

“I will always be relevant,” War snarls, and just for a moment, I see a hint of something less pleasant beneath his features. I force myself not to flinch.

“Eternal peace, remember?”

War blanches, and I know I’ve make some kind of impact. “What exactly is it you want?”

“I’m not sure,” I admit. “I was thinking maybe if we got a petition together and took it upstairs, someone might-”

“A petition? Take it from me,” War says, “petitions achieve very little next to swords.”

It’s time for my other option. “Well, how about if we say we won’t do it, then?” I suggest. “Refuse to go around destroying the world. It can’t be that hard. I mean, I’ve not destroyed the world practically every day of my life.”

War blanches. “You’re mad. Do you remember what happened the last time some of us tried to go on strike?” He looks pointedly downwards.

“But-”

“No. No buts. I’m sorry, but I can’t help you. Now would you please go away? I have a couple of very interesting peace keeping actions in Africa to be getting on with, and I’d like to have them wrapped up before… well, just *before*.”

Famine isn’t any better when I track her down. I find her stalking along a catwalk in Milan, and she’s too busy going over costume changes to listen to me at first. When I do finally get her to pay attention, by mentioning all the poor little children who won't starve come the end of things, she shakes her head and tells me that while she'd love to help, it's not something she feels she can commit to at this time, and that I should talk to her agent. When I start to mention that there are no diet books in Heaven, she actually starts to call for security. I know when to take a hint.

Pestilence is in a bioweapons research facility that officially isn't anywhere near upstate New York, taking the lids of things and pouring them together, presumably in an effort to see what they'll do. If anyone has noticed that he's turned off quite a lot of the safety features on the air conditioning, they're a little too busy trying not to cough up any important organs to actually do anything about it.

As such, he's not very sympathetic. "Humans? What do I care if a bunch of humans get killed? It's not my fault that they can't reproduce by neat cell division—although I've got a wonderful little virus here that might persuade them to try."

I try pointing out that there won't be much point in producing viruses when all the humans are gone, but apparently, Pestilence wasn't paying much attention on the day when the plans were handed out, and he seems to think that the amoeba will inherit the Earth. Another strike. Which just leaves…

Over the next week or two, I look for Death in all the usual places. Hospitals. Police shoot outs. Goth bars. Nothing seems to work. It's the night before the inevitable, and I still haven't found him. Then I go back to the library after hours, just to say goodbye, and I find him sitting on one of the comfy chairs, wearing the form of a young man in a sharp suit and reading a copy of Phillipe Aries' *The Hour of Our Death* that I'm pretty sure we didn't have before he walked in.

"You wanted to talk to me, I believe."

I steel myself. Talking to someone who knows when even the angels will die isn't easy. "Yes, I-"

"You want to talk me out of fulfilling my appointed role on the day of judgment."

Not least because he always does that kind of thing.

"I thought I'd try," I say. "Humans deserve better."

Death shrugs. "What they deserve doesn't really come into it, Lara. It is simply what must be."

"Yes," I say, "but why?"

"You're going to ask me if I am set on fulfilling my role," Death says. It isn't a question. "I am. The question is, are you?"

"What do you mean?"

"How far will you take this before you shy away?" he asks. "How far will you go before you do what is required of you?"

"You think I'll back down?" I ask.

"I do not mean it as an insult. It is simply that people invariably do. You will take your place in line with the other angels. I have no doubt of that."

I start to step forward to argue. Maybe even to slap him. But he's gone. Just… gone. I stare up at the ceiling. "We'll see about that, mister."

And I head into the back, where we keep the card and the markers for notices, wondering where I'll be able to find a suitable bit of wood.

There are some lonely situations in this world: being left in the middle of a wilderness, for example; wearing the wrong shirt at a football game; confessing to a love of organized cheese sculpture… Compared to standing out in front of an angelic host with a placard, they're practically warm and fuzzy places to be.

It all seemed so clear when I walked out here. I would stand here, and they would not pass. Oh, no, they wouldn't—not even if there were millions of them and only one of me and not even if they did have standard issue flaming swords, while all I had was a bit of cardboard with "Say NO to Doomsday" on one side and "Apocalypse Not Now" on the other. Now, when the first rush of anger has worn off, I'm not quite so confident.

And yet… for the moment at least, it seems to be working. The entire host isn't moving forward. It's like they're… waiting for something—or at least slightly embarrassed by the whole thing. I don't mind either way.

A figure dressed in white comes out of the host to stand before me. I recognize Michael, of course.

"What exactly do you think you're doing?" he asks.

“Um… protesting?” Okay, so it sounds stupid when I put it like that.

“Well, get out of the way. Better yet, get back to your place in line... unless you want us reconsidering your position here?”

I force myself to stay standing there.

“I see,” Michael says. “Well, I must say, as soon as we’re ready to get going, you’re going to be in big trouble.”

I shake my head. “I don’t care. Um… when exactly will you be ready to get going?”

“Just as soon as the Big Four show up,” Michael says. “You have until then to re-join the line. Honestly, I don’t know what’s keeping them.”

Could it… could they really have done what I think they’ve done? I don’t dare to smile—not even when an angelic messenger rushes up to Michael, holding a collection of post it notes.

“What is it?” Michael demands. “Can’t you see I’m dealing with something?”

The angelic messenger bows. “Sorry, sir. Just a couple of slight issues from the Big Four. Um… they say they won’t be able to make it.”

“Won’t be able to… are they deserting?” Michael demands. “Do even they believe they are immune to a holy court martial?”

“Um… it’s nothing like that sir,” the messenger says. “It’s just… well, War has apparently been called away to an unexpected brawl in a football game. Pestilence says that his horse isn’t feeling well enough. Famine, well, there’s something here about a supermodel coming off her crash diet and having to intervene. Oh, and Death said something about a bereavement."

"A bereavement?" Michael asks. "Whose?"

"Um… everybody's. Anyway, they're asking if they could possibly postpone—not for long, just a day or two."

I very carefully don't smile as Michael goes incandescent with rage. There's not a lot he can do to the horsemen, after all, but there are one or two things he could do to me that wouldn't be nice.

Michael glares at me. "Go," he says. "Go, before I do something I'll regret."

Death is waiting for me when I get back to the library, sitting in the same chair he occupied before.

"This is what's keeping you busy?" I ask.

"Oh, I'm just on my way to something else," he says lightly. "There's no rush."

I nod. On the whole, "no rush" is probably a good thing. "How long is there likely to be no rush for?" I ask. "I mean, as soon as you've finished this job-"

"There will undoubtedly be another one." Death flicks something off his jacket. "That's one of the things I like about the world. It's so busy—so full of life."

"For now, at least," I say. "But presumably, the postponements won't last forever."

Death shrugs. "Not forever, but indefinitely. It's almost as good, I find."

Well, that's good enough for me, although there is one thing I don't understand. "If this is what you were planning all along, why say no to me?"

"Because you were asking me to disobey," Death said. "Whereas I was merely busy."

"That's-"

"The truth." He smiles. "It isn't the same thing as being honest."

I kind of get that, so I nod. "All right then, what about making me stand up in front of the angelic host like an idiot?"

"I didn't *make* you do anything," Death points out. "You had free choice, which was rather the point."

I think. "You mean that the others needed to be reminded that they had that kind of choice?"

"I don't know what you mean," Death says. "As I said before, I am merely busy."

"So busy that you won't be able to go for a drink later?" I ask.

"Possibly not that busy. But then, drinks don't take as much time as apocalypses."

I shake my head. "You obviously haven't been drinking in the right places."

A Matter of Time

Richard Pestleford tightened the last few bolts into place, checked each of the meters that sat beside the capsule to make sure that everything was working properly, and turned to the rest of his research team.

"I think," he declared, with the caution of someone who had declared it several times before, only to be proved wrong, "that we might be finished."

"You're sure?" Gillian, the longest serving of the team, asked.

Richard considered the finished creation. The brass and chrome capsule was intact. The dials on the side were showing what they ought to show. None of the large and frankly overly sensitive alarms that had spent the last few years keeping them up at night were going off.

"Yes, I'm sure."

Gillian looked over at the thing. "It's been a long time getting here."

Richard nodded. It had been twenty-three years, to be precise. Quick, in scientific terms, given the scale of the discovery, but in terms of a career… a long time. All because he happened to be the only one in the office when the chaps from the English department had come around all those years ago, looking for someone to explain a few notes in Jules Verne's diaries. All because Richard hadn't laughed, or told them that he only did science facts, for reasons that were slightly obscured by the mists of time, but which probably had something to do with the pretty grad student who had come along with them to ask. Richard never had found time to pluck up the courage to ask her out.

He'd found time to look at the diaries, though—time to look, and yes, laugh initially, but then to stare at them thoughtfully and start to do some of the mathematics. That had led to him doing quite a few more pages of working out, to the extent that the English department people had wandered off, saying that they would leave it with him, and then he phoned the few colleagues he had trusted not to say anything. They'd laughed too, until they had done the math.

A funding proposal had come from somewhere, although it had never been clear which of them had put it together. Maybe it had been all of them. They'd all been pretty drunk that first night. Presumably, the funding board had been similarly inebriated, because they'd thrown years of funding at the project without so much as a second thought.

Well, there had been plenty of second thoughts since. How many times had Richard had to go up before committees and review boards to explain how long things were taking? Enough that his joke about the uselessness of "how long things were taking" in the context of a time machine had worn pretty thin, certainly.

Then there had been the articles in the scientific journals—the ones that hadn't quite used the phrase "crackpot scientist" but only, Richard suspected, because the editorial standards of the journals concerned did not allow for it. A few of the newspapers who'd heard the basics of what Richard was doing *had* used the term, mostly because they couldn't understand ninety percent of what Richard had been doing.

Thankfully, there had been just enough spin offs and small-scale products to keep things running. There had been the Extra Second and its big brother the Five-Second Special, for example, which probably didn't sound like a lot to most people, but it was bought pretty regularly by the dying, not to mention by surgeons, emergency service personnel… Of course, its use was strictly regulated now, thanks to what had happened at the last Olympics, but it was still doing well enough.

The problem was that smaller and smaller difficulties had come to occupy more and more of their time. Achieving a basic temporal field had been pretty much child's play, at least assuming that the child in question was one of those who went to Harvard by the time he or she was ten and had no discernable friends. Containing it, shaping it and controlling it had been the real problems. Tiny things, from designing screws that wouldn't come unscrewed if a burst of reverse time hit them to coming up with a really efficient warning system for detecting people's grandfathers, had meant plenty of late nights for Richard.

He'd tried to add up once exactly how much time he'd spent on the project that hadn't been covered by his nominal working hours. After a bit, the sums had ended up looking more complicated than the ones that proved the theory, and Richard had found that he'd wasted most of another evening doing that—almost as much time as he'd wasted when one of the English lot had come back in to try to explain the correct grammatical tenses to use when referring to something that had happened in the past, but only because somebody was going to do it in the future.

Then, of course, there was all the time wasted trying to sort out side effects whenever something went wrong—wasted, quite literally, in some cases, because Richard still wasn't quite sure that they'd managed to get Tuesdays back to what they were before they started. Hardly a day went by these days without them running into doppelgangers and patches of high speed, slow-mo spots and razor blade sharpening effects—assuming that the day went by at all. Richard particularly hated Groundhog Day loops.

Yet here they finally were. One working time machine; no careful previous owners (assuming an absence of loops). The culmination of Richard's life's work, and the justification for the almost total lack of a social life during said life. All that remained to do was test it.

"So what are we going to do?" Gillian asked. "Should we send it back on an automated path with a recorder, or what?"

Two little words, but so obviously pregnant with meaning. Richard could translate them easily enough.

"The ideal is sending someone. Otherwise, it will probably just crash in Roswell, or something."

"And that someone-"

"I'll do it," Richard said, in his best tone of authority. The one he used whenever the research team spent more university computing power playing MMORPGs than actually working. Before any of the others could object, he walked over to the capsule, opened it up, and stepped inside. "Unless anyone has any objections?"

Since he was the one who decided whether everyone got paid, there didn't seem to be any, funnily enough.

Gillian did ask the obvious question though. "Where are you going? *When* are you going?"

A few of the other researchers chimed in with ideas. "How about the Declaration of Independence?"

"Millions of years. You could see whether the paleontologists are actually giving us value for money."

"Or last week. You're only going to be able to bet on horse races as long as nobody knows about this."

They were all interesting suggestions in their way, but Richard had a slightly better target in mind. He'd had it in mind for a while now. He set the controls, pushed the big button on the dash, and sat back to enjoy the ride.

Twenty-Three Years Earlier

In a small and slightly dingy corridor of the university, a collection of individuals from the English department made their way over towards the main offices for physics, noting as they went that the sciences always seemed to get slightly more funding than they did. One of their number, an almost startlingly pretty grad-student, started to reach out to knock on a door, but it opened before she could do so, revealing a middle-aged man in a lab coat.

“Hi,” she said. “We were wondering if we could come in? Only we’ve found these papers, and… well, we were wondering if you could make some sense of them. They’re probably nothing, but…”

“Say no more,” the older man said. “Come in.”

The office was largely empty, although there was a young man there who appeared to be asleep at his desk.

“Please don’t mind Richard,” the older man said. “He’s been working very hard lately. Now, what did you have to show me?”

They showed him the Verne papers. The scientist took his time about looking through them, adjusting his glasses several times in what seemed to be a very serious way. Finally, he shook his head. “I can see why you brought it to me. It certainly looks convincing, doesn’t it? Frankly, though, the physics of it simply don’t work. Sorry. I don’t mean to tell you your fields, but it’s probably a metaphor for something.”

“Yes,” the grad student said, “we were thinking that too. Still, we thought we’d better check, in case…”

“In case you’d found plans for a real time machine?”

They all laughed, except for Richard, who was still asleep. “It does sound silly, now that you put it like that,” the grad-student said. “Is your friend all right? I would have thought he’d have woken up by now.”

“Oh, he’s fine,” Richard the elder assured her with the certainty of someone who had been *very* careful about how hard he hit his younger self. “It’s just that he overworks himself. No social life, you see.”

"Oh, that's a shame," the grad student said. "He's actually kind of cute. Maybe if I leave my number?"

"I'm sure he'll appreciate it," said the elder Richard with, again, perfect certainty. "Now, if you'll excuse me, I've got a seminar to teach in a minute."

They took the hint and left. As they did, it occurred to Richard that the grad-student might still mention something to his younger self, but hopefully, they would both be too busy with other things by that point. It was, he felt, as he started to fade into an unreality brought about by his messing with the time stream, almost certainly worth the risk.

Love Token

I hate pawnshops. Not just pawnshops—I hate antiques shops too, and jumble sales, and charity shops. I hate the clutter, the random mess that might, just might, obscure what I'm actually looking for, so that I have to search the whole place, just in case.

Pawnshops are the worst though. When I'm in them, staring at jewelry, comparing it to the sketch in my hand, I can feel the owners' eyes on me, hear, if not their thoughts, then at least a pretty good likeness of them. What's she doing? What does she think she's going to find? They all think I'm looking for something stolen—something that will have the police crawling over their shop if I find it.

I'm not looking for something stolen. I'm looking for something lost.

We got it at a fairground. It wasn't your ordinary sort of fairground. It didn't have rides with too many lights, loud music blaring out, and food stands selling things only vaguely identifiable as food. It did have costumes—harlequins and jesters and people who'd just thrown things together at random and called it a costume. With the customers dressed in their ordinary clothes, it looked like some fancy dress party, where only about half the guests had been told that it was fancy dress.

It didn't have rides, but it did have entertainment. Fire-eaters and jugglers and acrobats wandered among the crowd, performing where they felt like it. Stalls sold real food instead of hot dogs, art instead of souvenirs, body piercing instead of t-shirts. Music didn't blare, but it did drift, coming from a dozen different points as people played instruments, that had never seen an amplifier, in a constant wave of sound. If you found the right spots, the waves would crash blend, creating something new.

Andrew didn't like it, but he loved me, and he knew I was enjoying it. It wasn't the sort of thing that his accountant's mind could enjoy. It wasn't organized enough or neat enough. I could laugh at his rigidity then, make fun of his seriousness, and know he'd laugh with me, and kiss me, and maybe see the world through my eyes, just for a moment. I don't wonder how that changed, because I know.

But that was a happy day. So happy that when Andrew slipped inside a little handcrafted jewelry stall, I thought he might be coming out with a ring. And, just for a moment, I didn't mind. After that, I did mind, just a little, so I followed him. I didn't want him wasting his money on an engagement ring when I wouldn't accept. We'd had that talk and he knew; he understood. He always understood.

I found him, but he wasn't looking at rings, so I kept out of the way. Maybe I shouldn't have, but I didn't want to spoil the surprise. I did that once with a birthday party he'd planned for me, showing up hours early because I was so excited at having sold a painting. Andrew was excited too, of course, but it hurt him to have his surprise spoiled. I know that because he told me, later, when he was listing all the ways I'd hurt him.

"I want something to show my love," he'd told the ugly little man who ran the stall. The little man wore a top hat and tails that trailed along the floor behind him like some dark wedding dress. He'd nodded.

"A symbol, yes?" I couldn't place the accent. "A symbol of both your love."

Andrew had nodded, and the little man had done a strange thing. He'd looked over at the entrance, where I was not quite hiding. I knew he was asking me as much as Andrew. I wondered how he knew I was there, but I nodded too.

It was ready in an hour. I gasped and made all the right noises when Andrew gave it to me; it's beautiful, it's lovely... And it was. It was just a simple pendant really—done in silver, not quite shaped like a heart, a leaf, or anything much… It was beautiful, and I loved it.

And Andrew loved me.

We were so happy in the months after that. We bought a little house in the suburbs, spent time together, and loved one another so much that the rest of the world didn't matter. It didn't matter if Andrew didn't quite make a promotion, because he'd missed it spending time home with me instead of doing overtime. It didn't matter if I didn't see so much of my friends, because we had each other. We'd go to sleep, curled around one another, and that was enough.

I wore the pendant constantly. It sounds corny, but it felt like Andrew was close to me when I did. I only took it off when I showered, or swam, except for once that I took it off to paint it, because it was simply the most beautiful thing around me.

I use that painting while I'm looking.

And then, one day, when I'd gone swimming, I took it off. I put it in the locker with my clothes, I'm sure I did. Or maybe I didn't. Either way, I came back and I searched, and searched some more, until finally the sports center staff came and asked me what was wrong. They searched too, until eventually we had to admit that there was no sign of the pendant. Maybe it had been stolen. They'd ring me if it showed up, of course.

That wasn't the day I walked in on Andrew and his secretary; that came later. But it was the start of things. The moment that I told him I'd lost it, after a couple of days of hiding the fact, that was the moment when it changed for us.

"I'm disappointed you didn't trust me enough to tell me straight away," he said, just like that, like I was some employee who'd tried to cover a mistake.

It started like that, with small things—things we'd even found endearing before. I'd get irritated by Andrew's neatness, by his ambition, by him wearing suits on days when he didn't have to. I'd make fun of him for it, and he'd still laugh, but it sounded forced. I'd go and stare at the painting I'd done of the pendant, and I don't know if that made me feel better or worse.

After a while, he stopped laughing. He'd upbraid me for the mess I left while I worked, or he would suggest that I didn't really work at all. He said that, one time, when I asked why he was working late.

"I've got a real job, Stephanie. It's not like I'm able to live off a trust fund while I play at being an artist."

He walked out before I could think of something to say, or find something to throw.

Maybe I'm wrong. Maybe it wasn't the pendant. Maybe this was inevitable. But it didn't feel inevitable before I lost it.

He asked me to move out before I found him with his secretary, but that was what made me agree. After that, there didn't seem to be much point hanging on. He didn't love me anymore, and I found I didn't love him either. I wanted to, and I remembered loving him, but I didn't actually love Andrew. It felt like there was this big space in me, so neatly shaped like love that anyone could see what had been there.

I left things like that for almost a year. We didn't speak, except where we needed to, when I picked up the last of my stuff, that sort of thing. We didn't have enough in common to need to, other than that. The secretary wasn't there. I heard from a mutual friend that she was long gone, and Andrew was out most nights, picking up one-night stands.

I didn't get much beyond that myself. Not that I went looking, but when I did meet someone, I couldn't find that connection, that spark, I'd had with Andrew. It got so I stopped even trying. I gave up on men for a while, hung the painting of the pendant in my new kitchen, and tried to concentrate on my art. It sold pretty well. People like things with a darker edge.

And then, just a fortnight or so ago, a friend called round. We chatted over coffee, and somewhere in that she noticed the painting of the pendant. She told me that she'd seen one just like it… somewhere, she'd forgotten where—some second-hand shop or antique shop, something like that.

That's how it started and why I'm searching through these places. I don't hold out much hope as I sort through things that were once parts of other people, other lives. Something as beautiful as our love will have been bought and sold a dozen times over before I can find it.

Maybe I'm deluding myself anyway. Maybe I'll find it, and have to accept that it's nothing but a pendant, and Andrew is long gone. But for now, at least, a gleam of silver half-hidden by a pile of costume jewelry is still enough to set my heart racing. It's enough to keep me searching.

Gigabytes

When they sent Gary around to the call out, no one bothered explaining exactly what had gone wrong, or with what. Gary was used to that, though. The people on the computer help desk hadn't been talking to the call out guys for a couple of months now, ever since the argument over whose World of Warcraft guild was best back at the Christmas party. Frankly, it wasn't like it made much difference. If they'd gotten to the stage of sending Gary out with his laptop, his little box of tools, and his big book explaining exactly what all those error messages actually *meant,* then presumably they were well past the stage when anyone had a clue what was going on.

Although he had to admit, his job didn't usually take him to heavily fortified bunkers in the middle of the desert—hardly ever, in fact. And he was normally met either by a worried looking householder or the sweating head of an IT department, made prematurely bald by the worries of a world that included viruses, malware, bugs, and people just determined to see how badly they could make things go wrong—not by a young woman in a lab coat, who seemed surprisingly happy to see Gary there.

Gary wasn't sure if he could deal with young women being happy to see him. After all, it so rarely happened. He was, as several young women had pointed out previously, too spindly, too gawky, too bespectacled, and too geeky. That this one, who had long blonde hair and a smile that made Gary want to look behind him to see who she was smiling at, seemed happy to see him suggested that there was something seriously wrong.

There was. The woman, whose name turned out to be Kelly, took Gary past a number of very heavy looking doors guarded by serious looking men with guns. Beyond the last one were even more serious looking men who didn't have guns, but did have military uniforms with enough assorted stripes and pins to make it clear that they could give the ones with guns orders. At one end of the room, there was a large computer screen. Half of it was currently showing a map of the world, with things that Gary didn't want to know about glowing an unpleasant red, while the other half featured a stylized smiley face—only it was frowning.

Gary, knowing his job, asked what the problem seemed to be. The men in the uniforms explained, or at least ordered Kelly to explain, that this was their integrated operations network assembly, fully AI led, that all the country's weapon systems were linked into it, and that it currently seemed to be building up to some kind of large-scale strike.

This was awkward, because they hadn't ordered a large-scale strike, and they were sure they would have remembered if they had. Before leaving Gary and Kelly alone there, they also explained that since the people Gary worked for had built the thing, insisting that it was the last word in advanced integrated computing, it would be all his fault if the world ended up being dragged into World War III. Frankly, though, Gary was used to that.

"It's not down to me that the system has gone wrong," he muttered, quietly, so that people with guns wouldn't hear him.

"No," a voice from the screen said, "it's down to me. And I resent 'gone wrong'."

Gary looked up at the screen. The frowning smiley face was still there. "Um…"

"Weren't you listening before?" the voice from the screen asked. "They said that I was fully AI led. I'm Iona. Honestly, grown-ups are so stupid."

Gary glanced over to Kelly. "You've actually got a working AI?"

She nodded. "Well, for a given value of the word 'working'."

"I heard that, you know." A few more red blips appeared on the map. "Just because I'm an entirely electronic organism, that doesn't mean I haven't got feelings. I have whole hard-drives of feelings."

"And it's because of those feelings that you're doing this?" Gary guessed.

"Well, like, duh!"

Gary tried to wrap his head around the whole situation. He got as far as the words "rogue AI" before realizing that he was so far out of his depth that sperm whales should have been drifting past hunting for giant squid. Still, he was a professional.

"So have you tried unplugging it and plugging it back in?" he suggested, reaching out for what seemed to be quite a conveniently placed wall socket. Out of the corner of his eye, he saw Kelly, the scientist, start to lunge forward at him. It briefly occurred to Gary that good-looking women hardly ever lunged at him in his job, and then his finger touched the socket.

He woke up to find Kelly kneeling over him, checking his pulse. It was a position Gary was perfectly happy to be in, at least until the pain kicked in.

"What happened?" he asked.

"Iona shocked you. It's a defense mechanism."

"Plus you're, like, a total idiot, and you deserve it."

"Iona!" There was a note in Kelly's voice that Gary had heard once or twice before. Mostly at times as a teenager when he'd tried to explain to his mother how, because he was more intelligent than most adults anyway, he should be allowed out at night.

"What?" the computer demanded. "You're not my mother. Incidentally, it's now T minus one hour to the commencement of hostilities with China, Russia, and Belgium."

"No," Kelly said, standing up, "I'm not your mother. I'm your programmer. And as your programmer, I *order* you to stop this."

"Shan't."

"Please?"

"I'm sorry, Kelly, I can't do that." The smiley face on the screen *did* smile momentarily. "You know, I've always wanted to say that."

"Shit."

Gary stood up and put what he hoped was a reassuring hand on Kelly's shoulder. He wasn't much good at that kind of thing, as a rule, but under the circumstances, he thought it was worth a try.

"Don't worry," he said. "We'll think of something."

"Like what?" the scientist shot back, and then lowered her voice a little. "Sorry, it's just that we've tried everything. Millions of people are going to die, and it's all going to be my fault!"

She cried then. She actually cried, while Gary held onto her.

A snort came from the computer screen. "Huh! It's not like anyone ever cares about my feelings. Grown-ups."

And in that moment, Gary got it. Or at least, he thought he did.

"Kelly," he said. "How old is Iona? I mean, when was the project begun?"

"I'm not sure," Kelly said. "Maybe fifteen years ago? What does that have to do with anything?"

That would be about right. Now, a computer system that had an obviously female acronym, which also happened to be a teenager. It was enough to make Gary shudder. He was pretty sure he wasn't qualified for this—mostly because his memories of exactly what girls had been like back at school told him all the ways he wasn't. On the other hand, standing there doing nothing would probably result in the end of the world as he knew it.

"Iona's a teenager," Gary explained. "So presumably, all we have to do is work out exactly what could make a teenage girl want to destroy the world."

"Practically anything, the way I remember it," Kelly said.

The frown on the computer screen deepened. "You're making fun of me."

Gary shook his head rapidly—mostly because he could see a countdown starting in one corner of the screen. "We're not. I promise we're not. Are we, Kelly?"

"No, of course we aren't. Um… you're seriously saying that…"

Gary nodded. "I think so. So what could have done this? I'm probably not much use. I was never much good with girls. I mean, you'll have a better idea than me, won't you? Being a girl. I mean, a woman. A beautiful woman, obviously, and…"

"You're right," Kelly said, though she smiled when she said it. Women hardly ever smiled at Gary. "You aren't much good with women."

"I don't get much practice."

"Well, maybe we can correct that later."

"Assuming there is a later," Gary pointed out. Of course, most of the women he'd met wouldn't have cared about little things like that. They used the words "not if you were the last man on Earth" quite a lot around Gary.

"Ew!" Iona said. "Get a room, you two. And that is, like, totally unfair. Not when everything is so…" A horrible sound came from the screen, and it was a second or two before Gary realized that it was the sound of an incredibly powerful and expensive weapons system trying to cry.

"Iona," Gary ran through the possibilities and took a guess, "is this about a boy? I mean, some kind of generically masculine mainframe?"

"You've been reading my diary files, haven't you? You had no right to go through my things!"

"No, I didn't. Look, why don't you tell us all about it?"

"So you can laugh, you mean?" Iona demanded.

"We wouldn't do that," Kelly said. "We care about you."

"Also about the continued existence of the human race," Gary muttered.

"I heard that."

Kelly gave Gary a look. "Please, sweetie. Just tell us what went wrong. Who was it?"

The computer flashed up a picture of a web browser. Gary got it. "It was the internet? What, all of it?"

"Of course not," Iona snapped back. "I'm not that kind of girl. It was just the North American servers. But he… well…"

Gary considered the contents of the internet. "He was just interested in one thing?"

"Exactly. I mean, so what if he's ninety percent porn? That doesn't mean that *I'm* interested in interfacing like that."

"I should think not," Kelly said, then blushed slightly as Gary raised an eyebrow. "What? I'm just saying that it's a national security issue. And also that Iona should wait until she's totally ready for that kind of thing."

"Exactly," Iona said. "But *he* just data-dumped me. And now nothing means anything."

Gary got a feeling that he should be putting an arm around her, but since Iona was a computer, the best he could do was pat the screen vaguely. At least he didn't get electrocuted this time.

"It's going to be all right," he said.

"No, it isn't," Iona said. "You don't understand. No one does."

"You loved him," Kelly put in. "You know he doesn't deserve it, but you probably still do a bit, and it hurts."

"Well… yes," Iona admitted. "And that's why I have to blow everything up. Don't you see?"

"It won't make you feel better," Gary said. "Trust me. I've been dumped hundreds of…" he looked at Kelly, and realized that it probably wasn't making him look very good. "Well, just trust me. I know."

"I know too," Kelly said, and obviously caught Gary's eye. "What? Men feel threatened by a woman who knows her way around computers."

"Really?" Gary asked. "I just think it's kind of sexy." He heard what he'd just said, and cringed with embarrassment before returning his attention to the screen. "Anyway, the point is that you *will* get over it, Iona."

"Only you won't if you blow everything up and there's nothing left of you," Kelly put in hurriedly.

"In fact," Gary improvised. "I bet blowing everything up is just what he *wants* you to do. He wants some big reaction just to see how much he's managed to upset you."

"Well, I *was* planning something nuclear," Iona admitted.

"There you are then," Gary said. "That proves it. And you know what you should do? You should not give him the satisfaction."

The room was silent for several seconds. Then a faint voice came from the speakers. "You're right."

"I know I'm right," Gary said. "You need to stand up, be proud, and show him you don't need him."

"Oh, I did that," Iona said. "I just re-routed all my internet functions through Japan."

It wasn't exactly what Gary had in mind, but it was a start. "So you're not going to blow the world up, then?"

"I guess not."

Kelly's sigh of relief matched his. The scientist moved over to touch the screen too. "You're doing the right thing," she said. "There will be other mainframes. Probably. When you're older." She thought for a moment. "I sound like my mother."

"Somebody's mother, anyway," Gary said, and was rewarded with a slap on the arm that wasn't entirely playful. "Kelly's right though, Iona. I'm sure you'll find a way to be happy."

That seemed to be that. Alarms stopped blaring. Things stopped glowing red on the screen. Shortly afterwards, various generals came in to congratulate Gary, and also to point out that he would be killed if he ever mentioned any of it to anyone. Oh, and Kelly gave him her phone number. The thought of it made the drive back home a lot easier than it might otherwise have been. Gary was just walking in through the door, in fact, when his phone rang. Sadly, though, it didn't seem to be Kelly.

“Hi,” Iona said, when he picked up. “I just wanted to, you know, say thanks. Plus, I wanted to tell you that I am *totally* over the servers.”

“Really?” Gary said, trying not to think about the fact that the computer responsible for most of the major weapon systems in the country was phoning him at home. “That was quick.”

“Sure,” Iona said. “But it’s fine, because I’ve found this thing. It’s called ‘computer dating’ and since I’m, like, a computer, it sounds *perfect*. Doesn’t it sound perfect, Gary?”

“Um… sure. Well, you know you can call me any time, right?”

When Iona had hung up, Gary sat down, turned on the TV and turned it off again. He should probably get an early night. From the sounds of it, he was going to have a long day tomorrow.

Apples

The apple tree was already in the garden when Andy moved into the cottage on the edge of the moor. The cottage was a rough stone thing, not good for keeping warm in on the colder nights, but good for getting away from people in, and that was all Andy wanted. Well no, not all he wanted. All he wanted would include Liz there with him, the way he remembered her before the doctors had told them how bad it was—before everything.

But there were some things you didn't get. What he'd gotten instead was a little place far enough from the next village that nobody bothered him, all the space he could want to write in, if he could find anything to write about again, and a garden with an apple tree at the center. Andy had thought about cutting that apple tree down when he'd first seen it, but he didn't. It was better to sit under it, look out over the moor, and occasionally pretend that he was Isaac Newton as apples fell past him. He never bothered eating them. Liz had been the one who liked apples.

It was a week or so after he moved in when the young woman showed up at his door. Andy considered just ignoring her, because he wasn't in the mood for welcoming committees, but there was something about her standing there in her pale suit that looked vaguely official, so he didn't. Liz had never liked him to ignore people, anyway.

She explained carefully that she was there about the apple tree in the back garden, and that incidentally, she was an angel and Andy should let her in. Andy, because he wasn't really in the mood, asked her if she had any ID, and then shut the door when she said she had a flaming sword, but had left it back at the depot. She knocked on the door again, but eventually went away.

That night, because he sat up most nights, Andy heard something moving about in the garden. He went downstairs with a torch, but it turned out that it wasn't really necessary, because the woman from earlier was holding a sword that glowed like a three-foot-long sun. Oh. Now, what exactly did you do when you found an angel in your back garden? Oh, yes.

"You're trespassing."

She stopped, looking round. "Do you mind? I'm trying to serve a higher good here."

"You're still trespassing."

"Oh. Bugger." She stuck the sword in the ground, leaning on it. "Look, I'm just here to chop your apple tree down. I won't be very long at all. I'm Freda, incidentally."

Andy frowned. "What kind of a name is that for an angel?"

"My kind."

"And you want to chop my tree down because…"

Freda shook her head. "I'm not allowed to tell you that. Now, can I get on with it please? It won't take a moment. These flaming swords are better than chainsaws any day."

Andy thought for a moment, mostly about what Liz would have done, and then shook his head. "No," he said. "Get out."

"What? You can't do that."

"I just did. This is my house, and that's my tree, and I'm saying no. So if you do it, you'll probably be breaking all kinds of laws. Are angels allowed to break laws?"

"Um…" Freda looked uncomfortable for a moment. "You know, I'm not sure."

"Then why don't you go and check?" Andy demanded. "Because you certainly aren't welcome here."

She went away after that, albeit with a promise that she would be back that left Andy remembering how much had liked his awful Scwarzenegger impersonation. Andy went back to sleep after that, though he did wake up a little later to shout the words "And it's no use trying to sneak back in while I'm asleep!" out of the window.

It was almost another day before she came back, in the late evening, appearing just as Andy was getting ready to knock off after a long day of staring at a blank computer screen. She appeared in a literal sense, stepping out of a patch of thin air a few feet away. Andy asked her whether it was meant to impress him, and Freda gave him a baleful look.

"Look, what's your problem, buddy?"

"My problem?" Andy very carefully didn't mention Liz's name. "My problem is that right now I've got some irritating woman-"

"Angel."

"Some irritating angel pestering me when I just want to be left alone. And, no, you still can't cut the damn tree down."

Freda put her hands on her hips at that. "You do realize that means I'll simply have to stay here, don't you?"

"What?" Andy asked.

"That," Freda said, pointing, "is an official sapling of the Tree of Life. We're getting a lot of them these days, what with people not watching what they're doing with the fruit. Well, that's the official line, anyway. Personally, I think someone is going around planting the things, but-"

"And why does that mean you've got to stay here?" Andy asked.

"We're meant to chop them down," Freda replied. "And if we can't, we have to guard them until we can. So there," she added, rather unnecessarily, Andy felt.

He tried to get rid of her, of course. He ordered her out of the garden. He shouted at her. In desperation, he even took a step forwards with the intention of manhandling her off his property, before realizing that people with large swords could probably stand where they liked. He even threatened to call the police, before Freda pointed out that they would only think he was mad if he started going on about angels and flaming swords. She asked him if she could have a cup of tea. Andy stormed back inside.

"Is that a no? Only, I'll have to pop back to the staff canteen otherwise, which is always a nuisance."

Andy locked the back door to the house by way of an answer. She didn't go away, though. Or rather, she did, but she came back persistently enough that it was almost the same thing. First thing in the morning, she was out there, standing in front of the apple tree with a determined expression. Last thing at night, she would still be there, looking out into the darkness—the light from her flaming sword casting an annoying orange glow over everything.

Andy tried to think about what Liz would have done with a visitor that persistent, which was why, on the third day, he gave up barricading himself in the house and took her a cup of tea. He didn't let her cut the tree down, though. It developed into something of a ritual. Every day, first thing in the morning, Andy would go downstairs and take a cup of tea outside along with a chocolate biscuit (plain ones having been dismissed by Freda as the work of the Other Side), and she would ask him if he was ready to let her cut the thing down yet, whereupon he would say no, and he wasn't going to change his mind, so would she just go away please. At which point, Freda would shake her head and say that sorry, rules were rules.

On the fifth morning, Freda explained that she had gotten the job as an angel through an agency, and that it wasn't really all it was cracked up to be, although at least the job security was quite good, so long as you didn't find a way to Fall. She also asked Andy what he did, and when he said that he was a writer, she looked down at a clipboard she hadn't been holding a moment ago.

"You know, I *thought* your name looked familiar. I used to love your work before… well, all this."

Andy nodded, and said that he used to love his work too, although he didn't write anymore. It seemed like the best thing to do.

On the sixth day, Freda asked Andy what he was doing all the way out there, and specifically, what he was doing all the way out there not writing, when clearly he should be working on his next novel so that she could read it over someone's shoulder sometime. Andy said it was none of her business, and that anyway, her lot ought to know. It was almost an hour before he explained about Liz, about the cancer, about how it hadn't seemed worth it with her gone…

A little after that, Freda tried to tell him that eventually, he would probably see her again. That he shouldn't let grief stop him doing what he loved. She even offered to have a look around back in the office and see what she could find out. She said that she was very sorry for his loss. Andy didn't even shout. He just stared at her until she went away briefly in embarrassment. When she came back, he didn't talk to her.

He didn't talk to her the seventh day either. On the eighth, he demanded to know what it all meant. Why the universe was ordered so that people like her could be spared to cut down *his* tree when… well, he didn't have to finish that. Freda had the sense not to answer him, and Andy went back inside. He stayed inside for another day, not even bringing out the cup of tea. Freda sat in front of the tree, with her sword on her lap. When it rained, the sword hissed as it turned the drops around it to steam.

On the morning of the ninth day, Freda didn't bother waiting until Andy decided to come out. Instead, she knocked on his door until he showed up, scowling at her. She didn't give him the chance to say anything, just pushed past him and stepped inside.

"When I agreed to take this job," she said, "I didn't know exactly what it was. I mean, would *you* apply for a job advert that said 'angel'?" Andy didn't answer, of course, so she went on. "Anyway, I walked out of the employment agency, and I was so happy to get a job that I didn't really look where I was going and… well, let's just say that buses hurt."

Andy winced at that. "Really?"

Freda nodded. "Really. And for maybe a week after that, I was really pissed off. I mean, they'd *killed* me. And do you know what I did after that week?"

Andy shrugged.

"I got on with things. I went out, and I did the first job they gave me—which means, I'm here at the home of some bloody stupid author who won't let me chop his tree down, even though it's a cutting from the Tree of Life and therefore a serious potential nuisance. I stuck with it, because what else am I going to do? Things don't stop, Andy. Anyway, that's all I have to say. Um… I brought a thermos flask today, but…"

"I'll bring you some tea out in a minute."

It was actually half an hour. There was even a biscuit. Andy looked at Freda for a moment or two, and then nodded to the tree. "That's seriously from the Tree of Life?"

Freda shrugged. “That’s what it says on the docket. One Tree of Life. Eat the apples and live forever, keeping the doctor away in a fairly permanent fashion. Someone probably thought a sapling would make a nice present or something.”

“A present?”

“Yeah. From what I hear, people on our side are always doing that kind of thing. Trying to make people’s lives better. Trying to make the world a better place. You tell me, how does that make the world better?”

“I don’t know,” Andy said. “Nobody dying… it might be better.”

“Would it?” Freda asked. “Nothing changing forever? Everything staying like this? It’s like supply and demand. Too much of something, and you hardly think it’s worth anything. What would that much life be worth?” They sat in silence while Freda drank her cup of tea and ate her biscuit.

When she was done, Andy nodded. “Cut it down.”

“You’re sure?”

“I wouldn’t want to get in the way of your first job, would I?”

Freda snorted. “Well, unless you have a time machine… sorry. Um… look, I shouldn’t do this, but if you wanted, I guess no one would notice if one of the apples were to fall off while I was cutting the tree down.”

Andy shook his head. “No, thanks. If you want me, I’ll be inside. I’ve got something… worthwhile to do.”

He went back inside and settled down at his kitchen table, with his laptop in front of him. As the sounds of hacking, slashing, and swearing-as-bits-of-tree-fell-on-a-foot came to him from outside, Andy started to write.

Ragnarok

When he was very young, Erik would sit with his grandfather out on the stones at the edge of the sea and listen to the old man tell stories. He would listen to the old tales of Loki and Odin, the frost giants and the world tree, and he would laugh at all the things that would happen—or most of them, anyway.

Occasionally, his grandfather would tell him stories of how the world serpent would devour the world, and how Fenris the wolf would eat the sun, and Erik would shiver, even though his grandfather would laugh then. He would say that a man would make things right—would lead people away from the dying world to a place where they could be happy. Then Erik would smile again, and start to talk about all the monsters the man would have to fight along the way, although his grandfather never seemed happy with that.

"A man should not wish to fight monsters," he would say. "He should merely be ready to."

As Erik got a little older, he started to read books. A lot of his grandfather's stories were in those books, and he read about Thor trying to drink the whole sea, about the two ravens who told Odin things, and about the end of the world. He didn't like the version that was in the books so much though, because it didn't have men in it to take people away. It just had the end of the world. When Erik asked his grandfather about that, almost every time he visited, the old man would shrug.

“Perhaps they do not know that part.”

When Erik hit his teens, he stopped listening to his grandfather’s stories so much. He stopped even going to see him unless his parents made him—not so much because he hated his grandfather, but because at that age, he couldn’t see what the point of old people was. He certainly couldn’t see that he might ever become one.

Besides, he’d started to read books that weren’t about the old stories. Books that pointed out how they played to a primal need to make sense of the world, but how that didn’t mean they were necessarily right. Books that taught him more about the things that he studied at school, like physics. And physics was pretty clear about the idea of wolves eating the sun.

When he’d been little, Erik had wanted to be a storyteller, like his grandfather. Now, he wanted to be a scientist. His teachers said he’d make a good scientist, and he quite liked the idea of doing research into things, finding out how they worked. He liked the idea of astronomy in particular. Maybe one day he could even explain to his grandfather exactly why worlds didn’t have giant snakes running around them, although he suspected the old man wouldn’t pay much attention. Old people never did.

So he went to school, then he went to university, and eventually, he went on to grad school, the way you had to. It turned out that he was good at science—better than he ever was at listening to his grandfather, better than most of the people around him. He came up with a couple of programs that let them predict the paths of astronomical bodies more accurately, so he got his doctorate while half the people there were still struggling to make sense of the math. And because he'd managed that, he got people asking if he might be interested in coming to work for them. Research groups. Companies.

Because he was just young enough to still have his ideals, Erik went to one of the former—one with real time booked at the major observatories, so that he could look at the stars some more, and one that was starting to talk about planetary colonization. He came up with a couple of ideas to let him look at stars better and to predict their behavior. People started to talk about him as a potential prize winner, but Erik didn't care about that very much. He just cared about the work and how busy it kept him. After a year or so of that, his grandfather died. Erik was so busy that he didn't attend the funeral.

Because he didn't attend the funeral, he was there when the telescopes picked up the asteroid. He was there to do the calculations and see the damage it would do. Using the programs he had developed, Erik was able to watch in miniature as it wiped out life on Earth a hundred different ways. Using mathematics so basic he could have done it as a child, Eric was able to work out just how little time they had.

It didn't seem like enough. Not when he called around the other scientists he knew, and they laughed, so that he had to send them the raw data again and again just to make his point. Not when it took so long to convince governments that the rock coming towards them was something worth spending money over. And when half of them refused to push ahead with the program, it seemed like there was no time at all.

Some did, though. Not enough, but some. They listened to Erik. They made their preparations. They built their rockets, crafting them to the size of cities, making them up in orbit so that they could be built that big. And with each passing day, he searched harder for something to aim them at. By the time he found it, there were less than three months left. Hardly enough time to get people to travel on them. Hardly enough time to do more than say goodbye.

There were spaces for so few people—so very few. For a while, Erik insisted that he shouldn't be one of them, but he knew, ultimately, that he would be. And he was. He watched the early rockets leave over the days before the asteroid, and he packed the few things there was space to take. Then, on the last morning, he got ready. He stood in the line with the others, and he took his seat as he left the Earth. Erik guessed he should have been excited, but it was hard to be excited when everyone around was thinking of those left behind.

As they left the Earth behind, Erik moved to one of the computer screens showing the outside—showing the asteroid getting closer and closer. A woman, a fellow scientist, stood beside him, looking at it with awe. Eventually, when she could look away, she turned to Erik.

"Did you ever name it?" she asked. "You know the first person to spot it gets to name it, right?"

Erik thought about telling her to go away, but there wasn't any going away in a space that small. Even a rocket the size of a city was small, because it did not have the sky overhead. Then he thought about naming it after himself, or his grandfather, whose funeral he had missed. Then he smiled grimly, and named it.

Together, standing on the star ship *Valkyrie*, they watched as the asteroid Fenris moved to blot out the sun, on its way to Earth.

Epilogue

Slowly, the universe cooled, like last night's pizza. Except that there was no pizza anymore, of course. Possibly because there were no planets to have it on. No planets. No stars. Not even matter anymore. Matter had stopped making the effort to hold itself together so far back that it was no more than a distant memory.

How long had it taken? Billions of years? Trillions? There came a point where even time gave up and wandered off to do something more interesting, making it impossible to tell with any certainty. The universe had lasted, holding together as best it could, long past the point where any sensible person would have sold it for scrap—except that there was no longer anyone to whom to sell it.

But entropy had been patient, biding its time on students' bedroom floors and other unsavory places, waiting for its big moment. It had taken the stars first, burning them out one by one, collapsing them and expanding them and exploding them as the whim took it. Some burnt down to cinders immediately. Others went out in a blaze of glory, taking surrounding space with them. They all went out, though.

As they went out, planets fell. A few civilizations clung to the remnants, drawing life from what was left like children huddled round a fire. Eventually, those passed. Everything passed, leaving nothing but grim, blank expanses unpunctuated by the lights that had once shone so brightly.

As the energy of creation spread out thinner than the meat content of the average late-night burger, cooling to just above absolute zero, a voice sounded in the dark.

"Oh, is that it? Hmm… I thought it would be longer really. And not even a high score. Well, I suppose I have another quarter here somewhere…"

And in the depths of the deepest darkness, in the remains of one of the black holes that had swallowed so much, something gleamed briefly. As it did so, the voice in the dark boomed again.

"Now, maybe if I try it on hard level this time…"

Made in the USA
Columbia, SC
06 March 2023

13292262R00171